The Gryphon Generation

By Alexander Bizzell

ACKNOWLEDGEMENTS

I want to thank Trevor H. Cooley for sticking by my side and editing for me. Without him, this book would have never seen the light of day.

I also want to thank Vale Nagle for spending countless hours of his free time editing for me as well.

The inspiration for writing comes from Jess E. Owen and Larry Dixon. Without them, I would have never become a writer, nor would I have experienced such wonderful gryphon stories.

The gorgeous cover art, along with other fantastic images were created by Cyfrowa "Red-Izak" Izabela.

Front and rear cover layout was done by my friend, Scott Ford.

Table of Contents

Chapter 1 Another Summer Day

The alarm clock screeched in the dark morning of the bedroom. Johnathen's hand quickly came to life to beat the snooze button again and again until all was silent once more. He roused from sleep with a pitiful groan before sitting at the edge of the bed.

He sat, staring at the carpet, trying to regain any trace of thought. Suddenly, he felt a smooth and cool sensation on the back of his neck as something rubbed on him gently and a soft trill emitted from behind him. A little smile crept along his face as Johnathen turned to see his wife's eyes, still half slitted, shining green in the dim morning light.

"Hey there," he said before leaning in to kiss along her large, curved beak.

"Hi." A soft chuckle came from her feminine voice, trilling back to him before adding a yawn.

Johnathen found the energy to stand, feeling the cold wood of the bedroom floor beneath his feet. He walked into the bathroom and flipped on the lights, wincing as they instantly blinded him. He groggily walked to the shower and turned it on, adjusting the temperature to his liking before moving to the mirror. With his eyes now attuned to the bright light, he could see himself clearly.

The mountain man in the mirror was a mess. His black hair stood up in a twisted tangle, and his short beard looked as if it had been attacked by a blow dryer. He chuckled in the drunken state of early morning at his disheveled appearance.

It didn't take but a minute for the room to become steamy, indicating it was about time to hop in the shower. As the hot water hit his head, Johnathen gave a loud sigh, closing his eyes and enjoying the warmth running across his body.

He went about his normal routine of shampooing until the glass shower door opened. He squinted his eyes to find his golden brown gryphoness walking in on all fours, feathers just as rumpled as his hair was. She walked up to nuzzle into his upper chest with her sizable beak while the hot water began to run over her face.

"Did you sleep well, Thyra?" he asked.

The large gryphoness nodded, the fleshy edges of her beak curved in a grin while the water beaded over her brown and cream feather coloration. He ran his hands through her thick coat of feathers as the water began to soak into them.

Johnathen let the water rinse off the soap and shampoo from his body while Thyra simply let the hot water seep into her feathers. It was harmful to a coat of feathers to strip them of their natural oils. Only on rare occasions did she use shampoo to get the extra dirt and grime out when exceptionally dirty. The hot water soaking into her feathers made the room smell of her crisp, earthy aroma.

After a while, Johnathen bent down and cut off the shower. He opened the door, letting Thyra out first and then himself. He picked a towel off the rack and began to dry himself off. The gryphoness did the same, sitting on her haunches and using her gray foreclaws to grip the towel as she rubbed it through her thick fur and feathers.

Johnathen picked up his toothbrush and applied paste to the tip. He brushed his teeth while Thyra gargled some mouthwash. Standing on all fours, the top of her head came to Johnathen's chest. She primped and preened her feathers while he brushed his medium length hair back, adding product as needed.

"You need some help with that?" she asked, as it was traditional for gryphons to preen one another.

Johnathen looked over to the digital clock and frowned. "Already running late. I must have hit the snooze one too many times."

"Wow, I must have been out of it," she said. "I didn't even notice."

He went back into the bedroom, finding his clothes already laid out for him. A smile came to his face. It was the little things that she did for him that he appreciated the most.

He quickly threw on his clothes, working on the buttons while walking into the kitchen. Johnathen grabbed his coffee mug and poured himself a cup, adding a bit of milk to sweeten it up. He checked his sleeves and buttoned them up. Thyra walked out of the bedroom and made her way over to the front door to grab the paper.

"Great skies!" she shouted angrily.

Johnathen came to attention. "What's wrong, Thyra?"

"It happened, again," she said with disgust, her hackle feathers raised.

Johnathen walked to the front door to find the front deck littered in broken eggshells. The yolk had already dried on the windows and walls from the Georgia heat. The word 'Abomination' had been spray painted on one of the windows. Johnathen put an arm around his gryphoness to lead her back inside.

"Don't worry Thyra, I will clean it up when I get home," he said reassuringly while her bright green eyes looked down at the floor.

"I don't understand why they do this to us still," she responded, a bit of grief in her gentle voice. She tugged his arm away with a foreclaw and walked over to the couch, slumping down upon it.

Johnathen grabbed his coffee and walked over to the tan-colored couch. He sat down and wrapped an arm around her to bring her warm bundle of feathers closer to him.

"It's just Matthew's cult again, I'm sure. They are confused and scared that the world is changing but there is nothing they can do about it besides be angry. It's just how these people will always be," he said. He intertwined his fingers in her claws, playing with her wedding ring.

"Don't let those dumbasses get to you. They are too chicken to do any kind of harm anyways. Plus, who would be stupid enough to try to pick a fight with you!" he said with a laugh and reached up to scratch behind her long pointed eartufts. They flicked gently at his attentions and the edges of her muddy brown beak curved into that same beak grin he liked to see.

"It would be the last mistake they would make," she said with a chuckle, her feathers starting to rouse slightly as her mood lightened.

Johnathen leaned in against her for a moment, relaxing against her soft though still damp feathers. He turned his head to look at the clock. "It's about that time."

He sighed and kissed the cere right above her beak. With that, Johnathen stood up and threw on his black blazer, looking back at Thyra who had sprawled out on the couch. When she was stretched out like that her body took up most of the room on the sofa.

"How many deliveries do you have today?" Johnathen asked, changing the subject. He walked around the kitchen counter, retrieving his keys, wallet, and cellphone.

"Only three. It shouldn't take long. Not many people order groceries on a Friday for some reason," Thyra quickly responded as she held the remote in a foreclaw, using a talon to turn on the television hung up on the wall. "Don't work too hard!" she teased.

Johnathen smiled. "You know the law firm never sleeps."

Johnathen opened the door to the garage and stepped inside. He could hear Thyra chuckle as she watched the awful morning talk show she enjoyed for some reason.

Bright florescent lights flickered on overhead, shining off the two cars sitting in the garage. Toolboxes and pictures lined the walls in a neat row. His white Volvo station wagon showed the lines of a brand new vehicle, curved and slimline like all the modern cars were.

On the other side of the garage was a boxy old Ford Mustang the gray paint glistening with its freshly polished wax coat. The beige Mach-1 decal under the rear spoiler showed in sharp contrast with the rest of the darker rear end of the car. He itched to drive it. Unfortunately, that would have to wait.

His leather dress shoes clicked on the checkerboard painted floor while he walked to the station wagon. It beeped and unlocked itself as he opened the door and got in. Johnathen opened the garage door and started the vehicle. The smooth rumble of the small engine filled the garage as he left on his daily commute.

It was not a long drive to the office, but he enjoyed it nonetheless, especially on bright summer mornings such as this. The humidity wasn't bad yet. He could comfortably drive with the windows down and let the warm air whip through his slicked back hair.

The radio played one of his favorite songs. Usually, this would make him drum his fingers on the steering wheel and take his mind off of things, but despite the way he had shrugged off the events of the morning to Thyra they were eating at him. Sure, things like this had happened before, but that had been earlier in their relationship.

When they had met and started to date, many people had been disgusted by their attraction to each other. But over the years as the presence of gryphons became more commonplace, people had become more accepting. In time, they were accepted into normality. After their marriage, the hassling and vandalism had all but stopped and now for the most part, they were accepted as normal man and wife. But there were still the distasteful few.

Johnathen thought back to the times when Thyra had been forced to stand up to people shouting at her, calling her a monster, an abomination, and calling him a sinner. She had always been strong on the outside, but she had spent many a night curled up against him, crying, wishing that society would accept them. It burned him to think about the people still out there that would put his wife through grief like this.

"Damn it Mathew."

Matthew was a Bishop at a church cult that called themselves The Gathering. Johnathen had been brought up in The Gathering and had believed a lot of its teachings but as he grew older, Johnathen had lost interest in The Gathering and had stopped going right before he met Thyra. Somehow, Matthew had received word that Johnathen was dating the gryphoness and had made it a personal mission to force him back into line.

At first, Matthew said he was just 'concerned' and preached to him what the gospel said about intermingling races, but over time he began to get more threatening and even started to organize attendees of The Gathering to harass Johnathen whenever possible.

Over the years, Matthew had stopped most of the harassment, either from the restraining orders that Johnathen filed against members of The Gathering or just simply time itself, but little things like this still happened every so often.

Johnathen gritted his teeth and refused to get too worked up thinking about it. It was just eggs and spray paint. A bit of a pain to clean, but minor in the big scheme of things. He cleared his mind and tried to focus on the music, letting out a deep sigh.

"You need to concentrate on work today," he said to himself, trying to put his brain in the right gear. The firm had picked up a wealthy client, and he had a lot of work to do before the weekend.

§♦

Once inside of the office building, Johnathen called out to the secretary. "Morning Janet." He said, walking to the elevator. He called it with the push of a button.

"Morning Johnathen. Ready for the weekend?" she asked absently, concentrating most of her attention to typing on her computer.

The elevator doors opened with a ding, and Johnathen stepped inside. "Of course. It's the best time of the week."

The elevator rose and soon opened to his floor. He walked out into the main office room that was made up of multiple different cubicles of various shapes and sizes. People buzzed around in the morning meet and greet while the sounds of phones rang in the air. He could hear a couple standing in the kitchen discussing weekend plans over coffee as others scurried to their appropriate workplaces.

Johnathen smiled and waved at the couple while making his way over to his office. He set his briefcase down on the desk.

"Hey Johnyboy! What's going on witcha' this mornin?" came a rough, accented voice behind him.

Johnathen turned around to see a black-haired man standing there in a black suit and tie.

"Just trying to get the day started, Keith," he said in response. He did not want to alert Keith to the events of that morning.

"I hear ya got quite the client on your hands this quarter. How'd you pick someone like that up?" Keith asked with a bushy eyebrow raised, his scruffy little mustache curving up into a smile as he casually leaned up against the door and took a sip of coffee.

"Well, first you have to actually be good at your job, then second..." Johnathen began.

Keith leaned in to punch his arm teasingly. "Do you got to be a jackass first thing in the morning?"

Johnathen sat down and leaned back in his big black chair with a smug looking grin. A moment and a couple coffee sips later, Keith cleared his throat.

"Well! Kayla and I were thinking about headin' on over to that there new fancy place on west main tonight. You know, the new I-talian place with all them wines and stuff?"

Johnathen grabbed his own coffee cup off his desk and stood up to walk right past his coworker to the break room. "Oh yeah. I've heard pretty good things about it."

Keith followed him. "Well, the wife and I were planning to go tonight, and I was figurin' that you and Thyra could join us on a double date. After all, it is Thyra's birthday tomorrow, ain't it? Dinner would be on me," Keith politely asked, trying to sweeten the deal with the lure of a free meal.

Johnathen thought it over while he poured himself a cup of fresh brewed joe. "I don't know. Hanging out with you?" he said in a jesting manner while adding a little creamer and sugar to his coffee. "I guess we don't have anything better to do."

Keith snorted and slapped him on the back. "Okay, Mr. Uppity, I'll just tell them to make a table for four then!" he said, following Johnathen as he began to walk back to his desk once again.

"Alright, I'll see you tonight then. Just text me the details later." Johnathen smiled to his friend, and they tapped their old beat up mugs together.

It reminded Johnathen of their first days of internship together, when they were young. They often bought each other the most boring and mundane coffee mugs they could think of. It was their comedic way of saying they would never be uppity old white-collared men. They might seem like that today, especially after twelve years of working in this company, but they always acted like it was their first year.

Johnathen sat down at his desk, taking another sip of his coffee, and opened his briefcase. His eyes fell on the brown sack Thyra had placed inside for lunch. There was a little note and a dark brown feather attached to the outside.

Tried out a new tuna salad recipe. Hope you like it. Love you!

Johnathen smiled. Even after all these years, she still wrote him silly little love notes every now and then. He took off the note and placed it inside one of his drawers, adding to the pile of other notes Thyra had written for him.

His desk was nicely organized with various framed pictures of Thyra and Johnathen together. One of his favorite pictures was placed in the middle, the one of their honeymoon in the Alps of Switzerland. Sure, it had almost bankrupted them to take such an expensive honeymoon back then, but looking back, it had been worth every penny.

Just then the phone rang. Johnathen quickly pulled his cell phone out of his pocket to check it. Seeing that it was his new client, he promptly answered.

"Homer Associates. This is Johnathen. How are you today, sir?"

Chapter 2 Delivery

Thyra let out a loud yawn, her brown feathers rousing while she stretched out along the wooden deck. She relaxed on the upper balcony, overlooking the yard below as the sun rose into the clear blue sky. A horn honked from the street as a blue car drove by and Thyra quickly responded with a claw wave to the friendly neighbor.

This was her usual morning spot. She went up there to sunbathe in the crisp morning sun before it became too hot and humid to enjoy it. Before the patio was built, she had to lay on the sloped roof. She had begged Johnathen to build her an upper balcony for years before he'd finally caved in.

She chuckled, remembering how disheveled and exhausted her husband had looked after spending days in the hot sun building the deck for her. He had to read up for weeks on how to build decks and take multiple trips down to the local hardware store in order to complete this project for her. In the end, it turned out really nice, but not without help from his friends.

It was definitely her favorite anniversary gift so far. She used it just about every nice day that she could, so it wasn't like all Johnathen's hard work had been in vain. She opened her eyes again to stare into the pure blue sky.

Thyra lifted her coffee mug to her shining brown beak to take a long sip. She remembered many times when she had messed up and poured coffee all over her brown feathers. It was a bit difficult for a gryphon to drink from cups and mugs, but she had mastered it over the years.

"Spoiled bird," she mockingly said, gulping down the rest of the bold black coffee. The long black digits of her foretalons wrapped around the mug tightly as she set it back down.

Thyra then took the time to preen around her cream-colored chest feathers. She organized the feathers, thinking of the day's to-do list. It wasn't going to be that busy of a day. She just needed to do a couple of grocery deliveries and read some more of her book . . . and clean around the house a bit. Johnathen always volunteered to help with housework, but with the late nights he put in, Thyra usually took care of the cleaning. Which reminded her about the egg and spray-paint in their front doorway.

That thought made her stop preening for a minute, emotion washing over her like a light summer rain. Her bright green eyes stared off into the distance while memories of her youth came back to her again. Thoughts of people shouting and yelling at her came forth like a bad nightmare. She shook her head, trying to repress them once again.

Thyra breathed in the crisp air deeply, letting it calm her. *That was long ago, people are better and more accepting now.* She slowly stood up and grabbed her empty coffee mug. Then she opened the glass door that connected the upper balcony to a small upstairs guest room and went down the stairs.

The gryphoness placed her mug on the kitchen island and made her way into the bedroom. Her talons clinked and tapped against the dark brown hardwood floor as she opened up the closet door and stood inside for a minute, trying to decide what to wear for the day.

Gryphons didn't need clothing for modesty in the way humans did, but culturally it had become a necessity. A gryphon strutting around without clothes looked like an animal in human eyes while a gryphon in uniform tended to gender more respect.

Over time, she had obtained quite the collection of clothing items for every occasion, as well as specially made 'shoes.' This morning a mint green button-up caught her striking avian eyes. She grinned and took it off its hanger along with a matching pair of khakis to go along with it.

After a couple of minutes of fumbling around, losing balance once and falling on her back, she looked in the mirror and sat back on her haunches with a pleased grin on her beak. The shirt was loose enough to allow plenty of movement, but the pants were always an annoyance. She stretched out her hind legs and flicked her tan feline tail agitatedly. She liked to only wear shorts or a skirt, especially in this weather, but she had to look somewhat professional while working.

She let her entire body fluff up before shaking and letting her feathers fall back down into place. Her large hood feathers, almond brown and edged with light crème, stood up tall on her head before they laid down neatly again, creating quite the bountiful crest.

Thyra grabbed the gloves for her foreclaws that had been custom made to fit her and slipped them on, much like a human would do with gloves. She then worked on the hinds. She slipped them over her flesh-colored paw pads and used Velcro to secure them tightly to her ankles before standing up. She clutched her foreclaws into a fist, flexing out the black leather gloves. They fit nicely and protected her sensitive feet from being burned on the hot concrete, as well as keeping them clean from the road grime.

With her clothing situated, the gryphoness exited the bedroom and went to collect her work harness. She walked through the kitchen and opened the door to the garage. The lights were still on from when Johnathen had left. She let out a small sigh. He always forgot to turn lights off when he left a room.

Thyra then approached the wall where her large leather harness hung. She reached up and pulled it off of its hooks, then ran her talons across the etched designs in the leather. The metal clasps dinged and clinked while she inspected the harness to insure everything was in proper order. It was a complicated contraption and she had always found it a little awkward putting the harness on by herself, but she had learned to manage it just fine.

A couple of minutes later, she latched the last clasp in place. She then took the time to check the different pockets and bags attached to the harness, making sure they were secure and in place. After all, this was her only means of transporting groceries and carrying around all her other necessary items.

After one last inspection, Thyra was ready to leave. She flicked off the lights to the garage and went into the kitchen, grabbing her phone, wallet, and keys before throwing them in their designated slots in the leather harness.

The gryphoness closed the locked door behind her and made her way into the lush, green front yard. She stood for a second, stretching out her long and broad wings, letting them warm up and catch the summer breeze.

It's already getting quite hot, but that makes for better thermals, she thought and launched herself up into the sky with one hard flap of her wings.

A couple of beats was all it took to ascend to a good cruising altitude. Thyra stretched out her wings and glided with the air currents. The strong, warm summer thermals tugged at her primaries and kept her afloat as she watched the people below drive along the highway for their morning commute.

She beak-grinned in a smug pride, feeling sorry for those humans having to rely on a machine to get them places and not having the experience of flying free. Sure, there were less than ideal weather days when she actually coveted their ability to drive a car instead of flying in the rain or snow, but today was quite the opposite. She breathed the clean morning air in through her nares while moving her tail feathers to bank a little left, aligning herself to the first destination; the Village Market.

ᏮᎱ

Thyra came in low and slow to the ground, approaching the entrance to the large metal pavilion where the market was held every day. With a quick reverse flap of her wings she landed gently on the concrete below, which caused most of the people around to turn their heads. Some of them seemed surprised and shocked by her sudden entrance, while others only glanced before continuing on their way without a second thought.

She entered the pavilion through the main entrance, where many people were walking back and forth between the various stands. Smells of fresh flowers, candles, and baked goods filled the air. Some vendors had their trucks backed into their designated spaces, while others had more permanent stands allocated for their business.

"Hey there, Thyra!" shouted a rough-looking old man. His brown eyes matched his bronzed skin, which was leathery from all the years of sun exposure. It had always amazed her how a human's skin could take such a beating throughout the years and still hold up without any kind of fur or feathers protecting it.

"Hey, Jimmie! Just the handsome man I wanted to see," Thyra said with a little cheeky grin while approaching the large wooden stand.

All sorts of fresh green vegetables and brightly colored fruit were spread across the slanted stand on display for all the potential consumers to see. She sat on her haunches in front of the counter, chest peeking above it while she looked straight at Jimmie with her bright green avian eyes.

"Oh Thyra, you always know how'ta cheer an old man up," he said in an exaggerated tone, playing along with the gryphoness.

Without missing a beat, he stood up and turned around, grabbing a box of mixed veggies. He placed it on the counter and looked back at her. She looked at the box and rose up a little on her hind legs to inspect the order.

Immediately, her eye ridges raised in a surprised expression. She rummaged through the filled vegetable box with one gloved foreclaw and picked up the order slip before looking back at the white-haired man.

"This seems like a little much for Jessica. She usually orders a lot less," Thyra said, a little surprised and a bit irritated as she now knew this order would take up her entire harness satchel space. Usually her harness satchels would hold two orders, perhaps three if they were all small.

"Oh yeah. Jessica rang some hours ago and told me to double the usual order. Somethin' 'bout a party, I reckon," Jimmie explained to the irritated bird.

Thyra took a deep breath and sighed. She couldn't be upset at Jessica for ordering so much; after all, she was the best customer they had. The gryphoness started to grab the various items.

"Well it sure would be nice to know these kinds of things ahead of time," Thyra said as she loaded up on the various vegetables and organized them into their proper place inside the satchels.

Soon the brown gryphoness was all set to go and

Jimmie handed over the ticket with that easy going grin he always had. "Take it easy and don't work too hard!" he said, wishing her good luck.

"You know I never do," Thyra replied in a good-natured tone as she stood, testing to see if the weight was evenly distributed throughout the harness. At least it was a beautiful summer day.

She turned and walked out towards the entrance. The people around made sure to give her plenty of room to walk, mostly out of respect, but some were fearful of her.

Gryphons were quite rare to see, and there were fewer gryphons in the southern states than in the North. This was one of her most visited places in town, so most people that frequented the Village Market acted like she was no more than just another person, and that was all she asked for. Some of the people even waved in greeting to which she responded with a beak grin and a nod.

As the gryphoness stepped out from under the shade of the pavilion, the bright sun blinded her for a second. She paused to let her eyes adjust and felt the leather shoes become warm from the parking lot's black asphalt. Without the protection of her shoes and gloves, it would be painful to stand for long on the hot concrete.

She unfolded her curved almond-brown wings and with a quick sprint, she took to the sky once again with a course set to Jessica's house.

Jessica, an aging and wealthy woman, lived in one of the nicer neighborhoods on top of a mountain just outside the city limits. It was quite a long drive into the city for the residents of those neighborhoods, but it took Thyra half the time.

Her wings beat hard against the warm thermals as she pushed to gain altitude with all the added weight. She always found it easier to gain the elevation necessary and cruise the rest of the way, letting her long curved wings carry her along the wind currents.

She felt her harness vibrate quickly multiple times, indicating a message from her cell phone. Thyra reached into the small pouch located up against her chest and pulled the phone from it. It was a message from Johnathen.

Keith wants to go out to dinner tonight. You want to go?

Thyra thought for a second. It would probably be fun to go out instead of cooking. Especially since she didn't have any idea what to cook with the minimal amount of groceries that were at home right now. She flipped out the small keyboard on the phone and used her talon tips to press the individual keys and type out her response.

Sure! When and where?

After the message was sent, she looked up for a brief second and squawked in surprise. She veered off to the right as a flock of ducks flew right by her, barely missing a wing. They quacked out in anger at her while continuing on their way. She looked back at them and let loose a loud hawk screech, cursing back at the ducks in bird speech, her hackles raised.

"Stupid mallards," she mumbled under her breath. The phone vibrated again in her hand, and she looked back down to check the new message.

Reservations are for eight pm.

Good. That gave her plenty of time to finish what she had to do and get ready. She put the older phone away safely in its pouch and started laughing at the thought of the angry mallards that had almost struck her. It wasn't the smartest thing for her to text and fly, but those waterfowl should have watched where they were flying!

Next time, I'll have duck for dinner, she thought.

It wasn't long after that before she was flying low and slow over the streets on the mountaintop, heading for the correct house.

From above, all the houses looked relatively the same, which would usually be a problem when delivering to a new customer's home, but Jessica was a regular. Thyra knew exactly which house it was and quickly spotted it among the spiderweb of roads and homes spread out across the top of the mountain. She noticed that many cars and people were already gathered around the mansion, which gave the cheeky gryphoness an opportunity.

She folded her wings in tightly as she angled her long red tail feathers to dive down towards the destination. Within seconds she was close to the ground, and with a quick flick of her body, along with a powerful return stroke of her expansive wings, she landed roughly in a boasting display right in front of the large manor.

Several guests outside all gawked at her bold entrance, the backdraft from her wings blowing their hair back and kicking up dirt. A big cocky grin grew on her beak, and she settled her wings in, tucking them against her body.

She advanced towards the large door, and many of the well-dressed guests started to clap, as if it was some sort of show for them, which made Thyra's feathers stand up proudly. It was fun to show off every once in a while. The guests of the party welcomed this free display of her abilities as Thyra walked on by and proceeded through the open doors.

"If I thought you were going to put on a show for us, I would have asked you to be tonight's entertainment!" came a heavily accented voice from across the room.

Thyra turned her head to see Jessica facing towards her with a welcoming smile. Jessica was standing next to a couple of guests. Her dark brown-colored skin created a nice contrast with the white dress she wore.

"Well I was going to say you couldn't afford me, but by the looks of that new dress, I'm sure that you could," the gryphoness replied as she approached the woman.

Jessica bent down a bit to touch her forehead against Thyra's feathered skull in a gryphon's way of greeting. It was rare for the humans to do this with her, but one of Jessica's favorite hobbies was studying gryphon culture. She was fascinated by gryphons and sought out opportunities to practice traditions and normal social interactions with every gryphon that she met.

Jessica pulled back. "Did you see the young blond man out front? He's an owner of a second league gryphball team."

Thyra's eartufts perked up at the mention of the gryphball team. "Well you have to introduce me sometime! I would love to get some good seats or perhaps even talk to him about being a new player!" She said it jokingly, but in her heart it would be a dream come true to play in a professional game.

Jessica simply smiled and turned to walk down the hallway.

"What's the occasion?" Thyra asked curiously.

"Oh, this ol' thing? It's just a small gathering for a friend's birthday," Jessica said.

She motioned for the gryphon to join her with a flick of her wrist, the golden bracelets she wore clinking together as she did so. She led the gryphoness towards the kitchen. The vaulted ceilings made every step echo as Jessica's high heels clinked against the wood floor.

The kitchen was expansive, much larger than any one person would need. The antiqued, white-colored cabinetry accented the silver gleam of stainless steel appliances. Jessica

Alexander Bizzell

tapped her nails on the dark granite countertop, motioning for Thyra to unpack the groceries there. The gryphoness planted a foreclaw up on the counter and stood on her hind legs, now standing taller than Jessica. She balanced herself and began to work at the latches, which held the satchels full of groceries.

"It seems like a pretty big party to be called a 'small gathering'," Thyra said, putting the last words in air quotes with her talons.

A chuckle came from Jessica's red painted lips and she poured herself a glass of wine. "Sweetheart, if you think this is big, you should come to my sixtieth birthday coming up. You won't know what to do with yourself," she said with boasting grin as Thyra continued to unpack, pulling out the various vegetables and other fresh goods.

"I'll consider that an invitation," the gryphoness replied. "I'll be here, especially if there is free wine."

The entire kitchen island was now cluttered with various foods. Thyra let herself back down onto all fours and pulled out the receipt.

Jessica read it over and made her way over to a drawer next to the refrigerator to get her checkbook. "Of course, there will be wine, dear. It will be flowing like Niagara Falls."

Thyra couldn't help but laugh.

Jessica finished up the check and handed it over to Thyra, who noticed a green bill tied in with it. Her eyes grew wide and her beak dropped open as she saw the one hundred dollar bill with the check. She looked back at the smiling woman. "Really?!"

"Happy hatchday, Thyra. Just try not to spend it all in one place, you hear?"

Thyra quickly stood up on her hind legs again to rub her beak along the woman's cheek and neck, her feline tail swishing as she trilled out in affection. With that, she sat back down onto all fours, wings unfolding and folding again in excitement. "How did you know it was my hatchday?"

"I've got my sources," Jessica replied.

"Well, I'm going to treat myself tonight then!" Thyra said blissfully. She turned and walked towards the front door with Jessica by her side.

"I hope you do," said the woman. "Make sure to say hello to Johnathen as well."

"I'll make sure to tell him." Thyra said with a big grin.

With a little more swing in her step, she galloped into the yard, wings spread wide as she took off into the sky with an animated screech.

Chapter 3 Dinner Reservation

The garage door slowly opened as Johnathen arrived home. He backed the car into the garage and stepped out, shutting the door with a loud thud. He left his briefcase inside. It was Thyra's hatchday on Saturday, and he had all sorts of activities planned. He wasn't about to let work distractions get in the way of those plans.

He walked into the kitchen, breathing in the relaxing scent of the scented wax burner that was always turned on. It was Thyra's favorite scent. It reminded him of a cool autumn day in the forest as the leaves were changing.

He thought back to their long walks in the cool weather through the local park. Sometimes she would take off to the air for a while, circling around Johnathen and weaving through the trees for fun. Most of the time, she would walk right next to him, keeping up pace and chatting about whatever happened that day at work.

Johnathen set his keys down on the counter and walked towards the front door to head outside to the front porch. He frowned as he looked at the dried up egg yolk that still clung to the windows and walls from that morning.

"Damnit, Mathew! Damn you and your cult!" He used cult for lack of a better word. Most people thought of The Gathering as just another organized Christian religion, but its leadership was corrupt, and their teachings filled their congregations with racists and bigots.

For perhaps the tenth time that day, he considered alerting the authorities about this harassment, but he knew that would only stir up more trouble than it was worth. He decided to just shake off this little threat and not play into Matthew's game.

Johnathen walked around to the side of the house to retrieve the garden hose to rinse off the yolk that was stuck on the side of the walls. It didn't really take all that long to finish the job, and once he was done, no one could have been able to tell that the house had been egged at all. The spray paint on the window didn't come off so easily, though. He frowned, thinking that he should have stopped on the way home for something to remove the paint. It would have to remain for now.

Suddenly, he heard the sound of loud wing beats as Thyra landed in the back yard. Johnathen stepped off the front porch and made his way down around to the garage to see the gryphoness fiddling with the leather harness tied tightly around her form.

"Hey there, Feather Butt." he said with a large smile.

"Hey yourself, Slick Skin," said the busy gryphoness with a little grin as she worked her beak along one of the clasps located in the front.

Thyra then sat down on her haunches and used her dexterous foreclaws to work the other remaining clasps loose as they clinked and clanked together. "How was your day?"

"Oh, you know, same old thing. Just glad that it's Friday," he replied.

He made his way over to the brown gryphoness and reached down to help her with the last clasp. She stood up to allow Johnathen to pull the harness completely off her.

"What about your day? Seems the weather was nice for flying," Johnathen stated as he hung the harness up on the wall.

"It was a bit tougher than expected," she said in response and made her way through the garage and into the kitchen.

"Sounds like you have a little story for me." He came in behind her and closed the door behind him, then walked over to the large stainless steel refrigerator. He opened it up, grabbed two cold beers from inside, and shut it before making his way over to the couch where Thyra had already sprawled out. She took up a good portion of the sofa, leaving little room for him to sit.

"Yeah, well, nothing too exciting, but I did have a lot more to deliver than I expected," she said, taking the cold bottled beer from Johnathen.

Thyra placed the top of the bottle to her beak and with a quick jerking motion, popped the cap off. She handed the beer on over to him and did the same for the next bottle.

"That doesn't sound too bad. I guess that's why you got home after I did," Johnathen said as he took a sip from his bottle.

Thyra did the same. She had to put most of the bottle in her beak and tip her head back to pour it in, but it worked a lot better than trying to drink from a can. "It's not a bad thing! Just a bit unexpected is all. Jessica had a large party up there and ordered a lot more than what she usually does, so I had to take multiple trips back to Jimmie's stand," she explained. "Oh yeah, Jessica said hi."

"How is that old women doing nowadays?" Johnathen asked as he then sneaked an arm around the back of her neck, pulling the gryphoness over to lean up against him.

"More or less the same. Active as ever, even in her old age," Thyra said, still amazed by how old humans could live.

"You know, she's not all that old. She's gonna be what, sixty? She's probably got another couple decades." Johnathen had never met Jessica in person before, but Thyra talked so much about her that he practically knew her. He held his wife closely to him while he turned on the television for a bit of background noise.

Thyra shrugged her wings in response as she thought about her mortality for just a second, knowing that Johnathen would probably outlive her. There hadn't been a case of a gryphon dying of old age yet, but they did appear to age much quicker than humans. Science and medical gryphon studies were still relatively new, and no one had definite answers as to their life span.

"I bet your poor wings are aching, you unfortunate mistreated bird. I'm going to have to talk to Jimmie about working you so hard," Johnathen taunted, breaking her train of thought.

She chuckled and nipped at him playfully. "Oh, you ass. Says the man that sits behind a desk all day and drinks coffee."

Johnathen looked into her eyes with a big goofy grin. "Fair enough."

They enjoyed each other's company silently for a moment, idly watching the news before Johnathen asked, "How long have you been delivering to Jessica?"

"Skies, it must be, three years now?" Thyra said, trying to count how many times she had delivered to the women. "You should have seen her. All dressed up in this brand new dress. She had a huge party of wealthy humans with her too. Jessica mentioned something about one of them owning a gryphon league team," she said excitedly.

"I wonder which teams he owns?" he replied.

"Maybe I will have to talk to him next time, if Jessica

will introduce us." The gryphoness said in wonder as she became star-struck thinking of her favorite gryphon team. She'd been a huge fan of gryphon racing ever since she was a gryphlet. She was not the only one. Gryphball had quickly become the biggest sport in the world. It was shown on every sports channel, and all the other sports had now fallen to the wayside. "What if he could introduce me to some players?"

Johnathen couldn't help but laugh as she fluffed up against him. "If you do meet some of them, just don't go running off with one!"

Thyra's long feline tail batted against the leather couch, and she nudged her beak up under Johnathen's chin with a gentle trill. "You shouldn't be worrying about me doing something like that."

He knew that she wouldn't leave him for anything in the world, but it was always nice to hear her promise her love to him. He looked down at his watch to glance at the time, seeing that it was growing nearer to their dinner reservation.

"I think it's about time for us to get ready. Well, at least for you. It always takes you forever," Johnathen said with a small smile.

Thyra finished up the last of her beer and sat it down on the coffee table in front of her. The gryphoness then rolled off the couch and ruffled her almond brown feathers slightly, padding off towards the bedroom. "You can't rush perfection."

It wasn't long until the shower started as Thyra cleansed herself from the long day's work. While she chirped and sang in her bathing routine, Johnathen made his way to the closet to pick out nice clothes for himself. After a bit of browsing, he pulled a plaid button-up and a nice pair of jeans from the closet before laying them neatly on the bed. It was easy for him to pick out something to wear, but he knew that it was going to be a whole different story for Thyra. She did not have many nice dresses to choose from, but it still was not a decision she made easily.

For one, a clothing store that also catered to a gryphon's unique shape was quite rare, but it was even harder to find clothes in her size. Most of the dresses that she owned for special occasions had to be handmade and ordered from bigger cities, which made them extremely expensive. Johnathen had gifted her with many of these dresses over the years, but a good portion of what she owned she had purchased with her own money. Sometimes it would take her months to save up for a dress that she really wanted, which only added a personal value to it as well as a large price tag.

Johnathen put on his newly chosen clothes, and the shower stopped right before a loud blow dryer cut on.

The gryphoness fluffed up her soaked feathers as she maneuvered the handheld dryer in a foreclaw in quick rhythmic strokes across her face and body. Thyra was not a big fan of using the blow dryer and instead would usually sun on the roof on such a nice day to dry out her feathers, but it worked well in a pinch. It took quite some time to get all of the down completely dry. Johnathen patiently waited on the couch, watching the rest of the news and catching up with his fantasy Gryphball league on his phone.

When Thyra finally made her way into the living room, every feather properly preened into place. She was sporting one of her favorite green dresses that hugged her form perfectly. He smiled and looked into her striking green avian eyes.

"Nice choice. You always look beautiful in that," he said while getting up off of the couch and turning off the television.

"I know I do," came Thyra's reply, her long crest feathers standing up in display.

She followed him into the garage and he held the

passenger door of the long-bodied Volvo station wagon open for her. She stepped inside and sat down on the seat as Johnathen shut the door for her and walked around the wide vehicle to hop into the driver's seat. With the push of a button, the smooth purring sound of the well-maintained engine filled the garage, and he drove off to head downtown once again.

Chapter 4 I-Talian

Keith shook with laughter, slamming his fist on the table, causing the glasses and silverware to clink loudly. Johnathen laughed along with him as Thyra and Keith's wife, Kayla, gave them disapproving looks. The restaurant went quiet as many turned to look at the two making fools of themselves in public.

Thyra batted her long tail up against Johnathen's back, which got his attention. The serious look in her avian eyes made him instantly stop laughing. Keith received a slap on the arm from Kayla as well.

"Sorry! Sorry," Johnathen said in an apology, wiping a tear from his eye.

"Not as sorry as you will be," Thyra threatened as she continued to stare at him with a furrowed frown.

"Sounds like someone is sleeping in the doghouse tonight!" Keith exclaimed to Johnathen, which only gained him another slap on his arm.

"You keep it up and you will be joining him," Kayla said to Keith, just as irritated with her tipsy husband as the rest of the people in the restaurant. Kayla was the designated driver and being the sober one in the group had made her intolerant of the men's rowdiness.

The whole party was already a couple of drinks in, having just finished up their main course. Forks and knives lay across the red-sauce-stained plates, and Thyra put her empty glass of wine down on the table. She was seated on a soft pillow, which had been placed on the floor for her and yet could still see eye-to-eye with the rest of them.

Kayla sipped from her water glass, looking around the room as the boys continued their conversation. Everyone had gone on with their own meal, except for a group in the back of the restaurant. She had made eye contact with a frail looking old man several times throughout the course of dinner. The man would occasionally glare over for no reason in particular, but she seemed to be the only one to notice.

A young female waiter walked up to them, wearing a black uniform that was nicely fitted. She collected the wine glass from Thyra as well as the beer glasses from the guys. She smiled at the inebriated men. "Another round, sirs?"

"Of course! And one for my wife. It's her birthday." Johnathen said in a bubbly tone.

Thyra opened her beak to protest but the waitress cut in.

"Oh, I didn't realize! Well happy birthday. The next one will be on the house," the girl said with a smile and turned to make her exit quickly.

"John, I don't need another one!" Thyra protested with a slight chuckle, her head already feeling a bit light.

"Well too bad because we are getting another. Plus, dessert," Johnathen responded and handed her the dessert menu.

Keith suddenly looked up, his expression turning from amusement to concern as he stared at a man who was approaching the table. Johnathen turned around and saw that an older man had stopped right behind his seat. He stood, hunched over with a scowl on his rugged face. He looked upset, big bushy white eyebrows slanted with grimace.

"I think you should listen to your beast and leave here," the man said with a low grizzled voice. His hand trembled as he pointed his boney index finger over to Thyra.

Johnathen stood from his chair to face the scowling stranger. Thyra watched them, a frown showing itself at hearing how the stranger had just referred to her. Her feathers flattened against her body at the impending confrontation.

"Excuse me?" Johnathen asked in a warning tone to the taller man.

The old man was dressed in black, clearly a retired man with money. Johnathen had seen his kind before at the law firm, upper class jerks who felt entitled and set in their old fashioned ways. Johnathen despised people like that but had to work for them all the same.

Keith quickly stood to his feet as well, ready to back up his friend. The dark, low-lit restaurant became silent as people watched the scene play out.

"I think you heard what I said, young man. You and your 'BEAST' need to leave! I brought my family here to have a nice meal but y'all are making it very hard to enjoy it," the disgruntled old man spat, stepping closer to Johnathen as he talked.

"How about you hold your tongue before I rip it out." Thyra said with a dark promise. She stood, facing the man with hackle feathers raised. "Try calling me a beast one more time and I'll show you just how animalistic I really am!" she said, her voice growing louder. Gryphons were known to have a bad temper when talked down to.

The elderly man looked over at the gryphoness but did not seem threatened by her in the least. He stood his ground, dead gray eyes looking back into Johnathen's.

Johnathen held out his hand, trying to calm her down as he struggled to maintain his own composure. Keith had come to Johnathen's side, his arms crossed as Kayla sat at her chair, staring at them as wide-eyed as the rest of the crowd.

Johnathen looked at the self-righteous indignation in the gray eyes of the frail old man and took a deep breath, trying to find the best words to end this right. Part of him wanted nothing more than to turn this man's face into pulp, but the sensible part told him it would be wrong to attack a man twice his age. It was a good thing he hadn't drank more. Another glass of wine and he wouldn't have hesitated to knock the man's lights out, whatever the consequences.

Johnathen's body was shaking with adrenaline and anger, but he explained as calmly as he could, "Listen, we don't want any trouble. We are just here to celebrate my wife's birthday and my friend and I got too loud. I'm sorry if we disturbed you."

Keith looked a little disappointed in his response, having expected Johnathen to defend his wife against the extremely rude elderly man. The stranger continued to stare at Johnathen and Keith. "We were disturbed. Very disturbed. It's bad enough to have to see these filthy creatures running freely out in the streets, but now we can't even eat in peace."

Johnathen stared back into the cold gray eyes of the man, hands trembling with rage at the last comment. It didn't help that he was already tired after a long day of work, but this repulsive fossil of a man was really trying Johnathen's patience.

Sensing that things were about to get out of hand, Johnathen took his wallet out of his pocket and pulled out a couple of large bills before placing them on the table to pay for their meal. "Thyra, grab your things. We are leaving."

Thyra's wings fluttered and moved in agitation as she grabbed her purse off the ground. Keith placed his hands on Kayla's shoulders and started to walk her out. Thyra followed closely behind them as they passed the indignant old man.

"Have a good rest of your night," Johnathen snarled and was unable to help but bump the man's shoulder while walking past him on his way to the door. The gray-haired man scowled at being jostled and Johnathen didn't take but one more step before the man turned to say one more thing.

"You should keep that disgusting bitch in a cage, where it belongs. If I ever hear it threaten someone again, I'll have the animal put down."

Keith, Kayla, and Thyra turned around and the tension in the restaurant doubled. Johnathen stopped right in his tracks, clenching his fists. No one breathed. The next few seconds that ticked by felt like hours.

Johnathen turned and lunged at the old man, drawing back his arm. He threw out his fist as hard as he possibly could, and it smashed into the old man's face with the sound of cracking bones. The feeble man fell over onto the table, tipping it over and sending the glasses into the air. Loud sounds of glass shattering against the tile floor shook the room.

Many people gasped and jumped from their seats. Keith ran over to Johnathen and gripped his shoulders to pull him back from the old man, but he didn't find much resistance. One strike was all it had taken. The old man lay on the floor wheezing and moaning as blood from his broken nose poured onto the white tile floor. Glass and liquid littered the area around him, leaving everyone speechless.

Johnathen cleared his throat, "Don't you ever threaten my wife ever again!" he shouted. His head pounded, and he felt suddenly sick to his stomach. Everything was in a blur.

People swarmed around the limp man that lay on the cold hard tile. Keith looked around at the crowd, many of them with their phones out, taking pictures and videos of the whole scene.

"We have to go, now!" Keith proclaimed to the women, motioning them to follow. He pulled at Johnathen, urging him out of the restaurant.

Thyra and Kayla stared at Johnathen in bewildered disbelief as they headed out the exit.

Chapter 5 Aftermath

"What the hell, John!" Thyra shouted, shaking with anger and fear.

Kayla was in the driver's seat of Johnathen's station wagon, driving them home as quickly as she could. She wished it hadn't been her turn to be designated driver for the night. It was no fun facing the situation sober.

She was basically driving a getaway vehicle at this point, knowing well that the police had been contacted and were probably searching for them at this very moment. It wouldn't take the authorities long to find them. After all, Thyra was the only gryphon in the city that was married to a human.

"I couldn't help but hit him, Thyra! I couldn't let him say that shit about you!" Johnathen shouted back, his blood and adrenaline still pumping.

Keith and Kayla sat together in the front seat, silent. Tears fell from Thyra's eyes as she picked up Johnathen's bruised and blood covered hand, inspecting it. He had never struck another person before. His fist was various shades of purple and red. Later it would be throbbing and painful, but he didn't feel it at the moment.

Thyra was choked up, lost for words. She swallowed hard and leaned in to rub her beak up under his chin before sobbing gently. Johnathen placed his arm around her, bringing his wife closer to him as the tension-filled car headed towards Johnathen and Thyra's home.

❧

Keith and Kayla exited the car as the garage door began to close. Thyra had fallen asleep on the car ride home. Whether it was from emotion, exhaustion, or the alcohol, didn't matter.

Johnathen slowly got out of the car before reaching in and wrapping his arms around the sleeping gryphoness. Keith walked in behind Johnathen and grabbed Thyra's hinds as they lifted the gryphoness out of the car. It was awkward to carry the lioness-sized bird, but together, they managed.

Thyra muttered something, half-awake in a daze as Johnathen and Keith made their way into the bedroom with Kayla close behind. Johnathen and Keith gently set the sleeping gryphoness down onto the soft bed and covered her up with the large comforter.

Once back in the kitchen, Johnathen made his way over to the wet bar and grabbed a bottle of whisky off of the countertop. Keith grabbed two glasses from the cupboard before adding a couple ice cubes to them.

"Johnny, I don't blame you for what you did," Keith said in a low and soft voice as he made his way over towards his friend. "I was actually kinda hoping for it."

Johnathen reached out and grabbed an empty glass from Keith. He poured whisky into Keith's glass before filling his own. Johnathen was silent for a second as he put the glass to his lips and tilted it back, consuming the entire glassful in one gulp. He poured himself another round and held the bottle out for Keith.

"Thanks," Johnathen replied with a sigh as regret surged within him. "I know I shouldn't have done it, but what's done is done,"

Kayla opened the large stainless-steel refrigerator and took out a bottle of beer, then headed to the door that led out to the back porch. "Come on. It's better we talk outside so that we don't wake Thyra."

Keith and Johnathen followed, bringing the whisky bottle with them. Cricket sounds filled the air and a lighter shined bright in the darkness as Kayla lit a cigarette. They all took their seats around a round glass table in wicker chairs. Kayla puffed on her freshly lit cigarette and then offered the package to Keith. He took one from the package quietly and Johnathen did the same.

Keith and Kayla looked at Johnathen in surprise but accepted that it was a special circumstance. Johnathen had quit smoking years ago. Mostly he quit because Thyra absolutely hated the smell of smoke, but he also did it as a promise to be healthy for her.

Johnathen lit the cigarette and breathed in deep, letting the smoke fill his lungs and wash over him like a river. His mind faded and buzzed for a second as the nicotine hit him. He was remembering why he had loved it so much.

"I better not get into any trouble when Thyra smells smoke on you," Keith said to break the awkward silence. Kayla chuckled, but Johnathen wasn't in the mood for humor.

"I'll just use a lot of mouthwash. She won't find out," Johnathen replied and tossed back another big gulp of the smooth whiskey. He let it burn in his stomach and dull the pain, both emotional and physical. His hurt hand throbbed now that the adrenaline was gone, a stubborn reminder of his foolishness.

They sat in silence in the cool midsummer night air, the sounds of cicadas echoing in the distance. They dragged the cigarettes down to stubs and finished off their glasses, only to refill them once more.

"I would have done the same." Keith admitted and put

out his cigarette.

Johnathen contemplated a response, his mind churning over the events that had happened just an hour ago and the actions that he took. He would have done it again, the same way, every time.

"I know you would have. There is a socially acceptable line, and he crossed it. No man should ever get away with those kinds of threats and racism," he said.

"He got what he deserved," Keith agreed.

He picked up the pack of cigarettes once again and lit another one up. Johnathen grabbed another one from the pack as well before pouring another glass for himself and Keith.

As Johnathen lit the second cigarette, he felt more relaxed, more spaced out. He was beginning to forget the pain and the anger that he felt the more intoxicated he became.

"Now that we have that out of the way, you should know that this isn't going to be pretty," Keith said worriedly. "I'm sure all of it is already on social media."

Both of them knew what was going to happen next. They were both lawyers after all, and they had seen these sorts of cases hundreds of times. Johnathen took another long drag of the cigarette, his mind swimming with thoughts of the old cases and what was about to happen to him.

Depending on how a lawsuit went he could lose everything. His house, car, money.

Everything.

Johnathen took a deep drag once again and exhaled, pushing away the panic that rose in his mind at that thought. It was too late to think about that sort of thing. He would just have to deal with it as it came. He had to remain calm and collected.

"I know it's bad, Keith."

"I'll help in any way I can," Keith quickly assured

him.

Kayla sat silently in the night, not knowing what to say. Both Keith and Johnathen looked up at the moon that rose high in the sky on the clear night.

"Thanks. I'll need it." Johnathen said as he put out the second cigarette.

"Hey, maybe they'll spell your name the correct way and we can say they have the wrong guy." Keith jested with Johnathen, making fun of the mistake on his birth certificate.

Johnathen couldn't help but snort at the jab. The spelling of his name had been an issue all his life. "You'll never let my parents live that down, will you."

"Never. It will be funny forever."

Keith held out his full glass, Johnathen managed to give a small smile before raising his glass to his. The small whiskey glasses clinked together in a toast. With that, they finished their drinks.

Chapter 6 Hatchday

The morning sun shined brightly through the windows of the living room, filling the area with a blinding light. Johnathen groaned, opening his bloodshot eyes and squinted against the sunshine. His head felt like it was going to split in half, rudely reminding him of the previous night's decisions. His throat felt like someone had poured sand down it, and all he wanted was a cold glass of water. He slowly threw off the covers, finding himself on the couch in the main room tucked in nicely for the night.

I must have passed out, Johnathen thought to himself. He recalled sitting on the back porch for hours, talking to Keith way into the night . . .

Johnathen sat up and his head rushed in pain, scattering his memories again. He clutched his head, rubbing a hand through his shaggy black hair and found some comfort in the fact that his skull was in one piece. After assuring himself that he had other senses besides pain, Jonathan slowly stood up.

His feet dragged with every step as he made his way into the kitchen to grab a tall, cold glass of water. The cool liquid helped ease the desert that was in the back of his throat, and he consumed the whole thing in one motion.

As he sat the glass down he heard the crashing of glasses in his memory. He looked down at his hand, noticing the discoloration on his knuckles, and saw the foul old man's stunned and bloody face looking back up at him. It all came back to him in a wave. He turned to stare blankly out the kitchen window, his heart sinking into his chest. He stood for a minute, replaying the memory again and again before taking a deep breath.

"Thyra," he said with a grimace, recalling her tears from last night and how she had fallen asleep in the car. He remembered carrying her with Keith into the bedroom.

Johnathen quickly sneaked over to the bedroom door, careful to not make too much noise. He peeked his head inside to find the golden-brown gryphoness still fast asleep on the bed, sprawled out across the mattress with the covers flung about everywhere. Johnathen watched her for a moment, relieved to see her sound asleep.

There was still time to make her hatchday breakfast and perhaps make up for the disastrous dinner the night before.

Johnathen eased the oak door shut before making his way into the kitchen. His stomach ached, and he felt nauseous. It was hard to concentrate on even simple tasks, but he managed. He grabbed a couple of pans out of the cupboard, along with some eggs and bacon from the fridge.

It was simple enough to cook the bacon and eggs, but there was one thing that Thyra loved for breakfast, fresh salmon. Johnathen had purchased some from the market the day before and had it wrapped up in the fridge. He pulled out the fish and put it on a cutting board. Taking a knife in hand, he carefully cut off thin slivers of pink salmon flesh as his hands trembled.

The kitchen was soon filled with the heavy aroma of sizzling and popping bacon. He plated everything on a large serving dish and cut off the gas burning eyes of the stovetop. He placed the prepared plate on a bed-serving tray that he had bought for this very occasion. Satisfied with his work, he made his way over to the bedroom door once again, tray in hand.

Thyra was still sound asleep inside, her tail hanging limply out of the covers at the edge of the bed, dragging along the floor. Johnathen sat on the edge of the bed and placed the tray upon the dark-colored wooden nightstand.

"Thyra," he said in a low gentle voice, drawing out the word for a second and running his fingers through her thick chest plumage. There was a slight stir as the large gryphoness rumbled something and rolled gently. Her eyes were still closed in the darkened room, but he could clearly see a little beak grin on her face.

"Hey you," Thyra greeted him in a sluggish trilling voice, still trying to wake up from her deep slumber. Johnathen continued to rub through the golden brown plumage, ruffling her already disheveled feathers.

"Hey there. How do you feel?" he asked gently, wondering if she felt anywhere near as bad as he did this morning. Though it was rare for her to have any sort of hangover as her body processed alcohol at a quicker rate than that of any human. The metabolism of a gryphon was something to behold, especially when they were flying for most of the day.

Thyra let out a gentle rumble from her throat, stretching a little bit on the bed. Her piercing green eyes slowly opened, the events of the previous night coming back to memory. Her brow furrowed. "Just dandy."

Johnathen heard the concerned tone in her voice. "I made your favorite," he said, changing the subject. He lifted his hand off of her chest and pulled the tray closer to her on the nightstand. Thyra's eyes grew wide in excitement at the sight of the delicious food plated out for her.

Thyra started to say something but before she could get a word out, Johnathen leaned in and placed a kiss upon her smooth beak.

"Happy hatchday," he said with a grin, standing back up once again to give her room to eat. Thyra picked up the fork and chirped with glee before digging right into the cheesy eggs, garnished with the fresh slices of salmon.

"You know salmon is my favorite," the gryphoness exclaimed before taking a large bite of the delicacy.

Johnathen smiled, watching her take a bite. "Of course, I do. What kind of a husband would I be if I didn't know my wife's favorite breakfast food?"

Thyra chuckled, momentarily forgetting about the night's previous events as she began to devour the breakfast before her.

He turned and headed out the door, making his way to the kitchen. Moments later a loud pop echoed across the house, making Thyra's long eartufts perk. He walked back into the room, holding a large glass of bubbling orange juice. Thyra smiled at him, a little egg hanging from her beak. She knew exactly what the glass contained. It was a mimosa.

Early on in their relationship, they always met at the same restaurant on Sunday afternoon brunch. It would not matter how busy he was that week or whatever was going on, Johnathen always made sure to be there. They had spent countless hours on the restaurant's patio, sharing conversations and enjoying the mimosas. It continued to be a tradition for many years, and the sight of the bubbly orange beverage brought her back.

"Going all out for me today, aren't you?" she said, swallowing down another helping of eggs and salmon. She reached out and took the glass from him, holding it to her beak. The glass was formed in an elongated oval shape made especially for a gryphon's use.

"You know it. Everything for my darling bird," he said. "I even used the twenty dollar champagne for it."

She finished her sip of the orange concoction and chuckled. "Oh my, pulling out all the stops. Sure we can afford that?"

"I had to take out a second mortgage, but we should be fine," he retorted, sitting down on the bed next to her.

Thyra picked up one of the slices of crispy bacon, happily munching on it to savor the greasy flavor. Johnathen reached over to steal a slice for himself and she playfully batted his hand aside with one of her foreclaws.

Johnathen winced as the claw scraped across his injured hand. Thyra's eartufts folded back at the reminder of the night before, and her beak grin turned into a frown. She stared down at the empty plate, thinking about everything that had happened last night, and what that meant for his future.

Johnathen still stole the piece of bacon and put it into his mouth before he noticed the sudden change in her mood. He reached over and caressed her feathered cheek in his palm. He lifted her head gently so he that could look her in the eyes again. "What's wrong Thyra?"

"It's…it's just that I was thinking about what happened. H-how you hit that man. And what is going to happen now. And-."

"Thyra, don't worry about it. Let me handle it," Johnathen cut into her train of thought, trying to calm her down.

She looked down once again, and he continued to rub her cheek for a minute. He always tried to remain optimistic, so as to not worry her too much. He grabbed the tray, then stood up and made his way back into the kitchen.

Thyra took another sip of the bubbly orange juice, finishing it off in the last gulp, and slowly stood up and slid out of bed. She lowered her chest down to the ground, arched her back up and spread out her wings. A loud yawn came from her open beak and her body shivered as she stretched her toned muscles back to life.

She still could not stop worrying about what was going to become of his actions from last night. Sure, Johnathen acted like it was nothing, but assault was not something that this conservative town would take lightly, especially since the victim was an elderly man.

"So, I've got a surprise for you later today," Johnathen yelled from the kitchen, breaking up her depressing thoughts.

"Oh? Do you now?" she asked in a curious tone, having to raise her voice over the sound of water from the kitchen sink. She padded into the kitchen to join him.

"I do. And something tells me you're going to love it," he stated, excited about the day's plans.

Johnathen washed the pans and the platter quickly before placing them into the open dishwasher. Thyra had already grabbed hold of the bottle of champagne and was making herself a fresh glass. Johnathen unscrewed the lid to the orange juice and added it to her cup.

"Well, what is it then?" she asked, looking up at him curiously.

Johnathen finished up the pouring and put the lid back on. "It's a surprise." He stated quite bluntly, giving the gryphoness a little grin while he put the container back into the refrigerator.

"I see how it is," she retorted, turning around and flicking her feline tail at him. She made her way to the couch, carrying the full glass in a free foreclaw. She had to limp a bit on the remaining three feet, but after years of practice, she had become used to it and didn't spill a drop. She made herself comfortable on the sofa and sipped from her glass while Johnathen busied himself cleaning the grease off of the glass stovetop on the island table.

Thyra switched on the large TV with the remote, scrolling through the channels until she found something about the big gryphball game happening that night.

"Well, whatever you have planned, just make sure we are back home to watch the game! The Jacksonville Kites are playing against the Atlanta Ospreys and I can't miss that!" she exclaimed.

"I promise you won't miss the game tonight," Johnathen replied, a big grin growing on his face.

The Kites and the Ospreys were in the finals, and the winner would go on to play in the Silver Wing. It was the final game of the year and he had already received extremely good seats for her. It was the perfect gift and they had not been easy to obtain.

The game had been sold out for weeks, but he had known that Jessica, the wealthy woman Thyra delivered to, had a lot of connections. He had asked Jessica to do him a favor and sure enough, she knew someone that not only had ways of getting the tickets, but just happened to be the man Thyra had mentioned before who also owned a minor league gryphon team.

The man's name was Richard. Johnathen had met with him a couple nights previously in his large mansion on top of the mountain. Richard had been happy to meet with Jonathan and was even willing to give him the tickets free of charge. On one condition.

Richard had seen Thyra fly several times in the past during her deliveries to Jessica, and he wished to speak with the gryphon. Johnathen wasn't too sure what it was about, but he had agreed to set up dinner plans for later in the week.

He would talk to Thyra about that later, but for now, they had a game to catch.

Chapter 7 Semi-Finals

A loud screech of excitement rang in Jonathan's ears, causing him to wince despite the wide smile on his face. The small confines of the car only magnified Thyra's hawk call. She was bouncing up and down in her seat, fluffing up her feathers and chirping with glee as she saw the large sign depicting an image of the racing stadium. All his efforts on obtaining those tickets paid off right then and there.

"Are . . . are we really going to the game?!" she asked excitedly, the crest feathers on her head standing straight up. The gryphoness could barely get the words out.

"I told you that you were going to love your surprise."

Thyra couldn't hold still for the life of her. She had always been excited when she was able to go see a game, even the minor leagues, but to attend the professional finals game was a dream she'd had ever since she was a gryphlet. "H-how did you even pull this off? This game has been sold out since day one!"

"Let's just say, I have my connections." With that response, he pulled into the overcrowded parking lot. There were cars everywhere, along with people in brightly-colored jackets herding him towards an open spot. The large domed structure of the stadium loomed over them, casting a shadow that engulfed most of the parking lot in the evening sun.

"This new stadium is even bigger than the old one!" Thyra exclaimed, hopping out of the car as soon as they came to a stop. As gryphball had become more popular, the stadiums had become bigger and better. This current monstrosity had an automatic retractable dome, making it as expensive as any NFL stadium.

Johnathen shut the car door behind him, watching her prance around the parking area with glee. He couldn't help but laugh as his overly-excited wife made a fool of herself in public.

A little boy ran out from between a couple parked cars, holding a picture and a marker in one hand. He approached Thyra and tugged at her wing feathers, causing her to quickly turn her head towards him. The boy had freckles all over his face and pasty white skin and had to look way up to look Thyra in the eyes. The little boy's brown eyes were huge, like he was looking at a movie star and his big grin stretched from cheek to cheek as he held out the picture and the marker.

Thyra was legitimately confused by the boy's reaction to seeing her. She turned her body completely around before sitting down on her haunches in front of the red-headed child. His parents quickly followed, surveying the scene while Johnathen also made his way over, just as curious as Thyra was.

"I...I'm a big fan!" he yelled and shook his picture at Thyra, wanting her to grab it from him.

She took the picture from the little boy in her talons, holding it so she could actually see the image. It was a picture of Tyler Smith, the front flyer of the Jacksonville kites. Thyra chuckled at the little boy's mistake. She did share similar feather coloration with Tyler and on the TV screen it was hard to tell, but Tyler was actually larger than she was.

"We are so sorry!" The father of the little boy expressed, making his way over to grab his son's hand.

"Oh, not to worry, he wasn't bothering me at all." She grinned down at the little boy and carefully grabbed the marker with her large talons. She had seen Tyler Smith's signature before and tried her best to replicate it.

Done with her handiwork, she handed the picture and pen back to the boy. He took it and gasped in amazement at obtaining his favorite player's signature. Even though the signature was from Thyra's talons instead of the star flier, it was real to him.

"Can you do me a favor?" she asked the little boy, who clearly was buying the whole act. He pulled on his dad's hand and quickly nodded in response. "I want you to cheer loud for the Kites today, got it?"

The pasty white boy laughed and gave a big thumbs up to Thyra. "Yeah! I will!"

The parents were pleased with the whole act, mouthing the words thank you to Thyra. She gave a wink and a nod before they started to walk away. The little boy turned to look at his star once more before grinning and taking off towards the stadium.

Johnathen came to stand next to Thyra and wrapped an arm around her neck, pulling her close. "You know, you probably just made that little guy's day. It'll be something he will remember for a long time."

"I didn't know what else to do! I didn't want to be rude and break the little boy's heart," Thyra replied. She stood up onto all fours and began to walk towards the front gate.

"Well, I thought it was hilarious, and you put on one hell of a convincing act! I could have sworn I was looking at the amazing Tyler Smith!" Jonathan mocked Thyra playfully, reaching into his pockets to grab the tickets. She huffed through her nares and shoved him playfully. He stumbled a bit and laughed.

She snorted, "They must not have any gryphons where he comes from. He apparently can't tell the difference between a hen and a drake."

"It could have been the whole fact that he was about five years old." He suggested.

"Forgive me for not being able to tell the age of young humans! They all look the same to me." Thyra retorted. She had a hard time guessing the age of any person, not just the young and the elderly.

They approached the gate and joined one of the several long lines of people waiting to get through the gates. Guards were checking personal belongings and scanning tickets to allow them through.

Thyra could not remember the last time she had seen so many people in one place like this. Many people turned their heads to look at the gryphoness standing right next to them. Most did not mind her presence and acted like it was a normal thing, but there were a couple that made a little extra room between themselves and her.

It didn't take long until they were inside. The hallway beyond the entrance opened up into a wide midway, surrounded by shops and vendors on either side. Gigantic television screens had been hung periodically above the shops, displaying footage of the player gryphons practicing for the game.

People went back and forth in front of her, some taking a couple glances at the gryphon as they walked by heading towards their seats. She even saw another gryphon or two in the area, which made her fluff up with glee. It was rare to run into another gryphon in Macon, and it was always a welcome sight to see her own kind.

Johnathen approached one of the bigger shops off to the side and opened the door to let Thyra in. Clothing, hats, and all sorts of Atlanta Ospreys knickknacks decorated the store. Kids and adults alike were at the register, buying their favorite player's jersey or a little bobble head commemorative. Johnathen picked up a hat off of the wall and placed it on top of Thyra's head. She pinned her ears back as it sat awkwardly on top of her head, which made him chuckle.

"Looks good on you," he commented, making Thyra laugh.

"I look good in anything! It just doesn't fit me right. Probably because of the whole fact it was made for people," Thyra replied, taking off the hat and hanging it back up on the wall. She began to walk around the store as Johnathen browsed, picking up an ugly blue-and-yellow lamp with a gryphon flying on the front.

She found the small section that had different jerseys and hats made specifically for gryphons. Among them was Tyler Smith's jersey, number twenty six. The gryphoness couldn't help but pick the replica jersey off the wall. She sat on her haunches, slinging the shirt around her back and guiding her wings through the large openings in the back of the jersey. Thyra put her scaled arms through the armholes and started to button it up on her chest.

She looked at herself in the mirror and grinned. Now she looked like a proper fan. The blue button up jersey with gold lettering didn't look half bad on her! Johnathen walked up from behind, smiling as Thyra observed herself in the mirror.

"That's a good fit on you." Johnathen said, then picked up a gryphon fitted hat from the shelf and put it on Thyra's head.

Her crest feathers crunched down under the dome, but it still fit quite nicely. The holes in the top of the hat were big enough to put her eartufts through. It had the Kites logo displayed on the front, which only added to her fan garb.

" You're right, it does fit pretty nicely. I like it," Thyra commented and ran her claws along the slick mesh of the fake jersey. She found the tag and took a peek at the price.

"Great Skies! It doesn't look a hundred dollars good, though," the gryphon exclaimed.

Johnathen shrugged. "It's your hatchday after all. If you want it, you can have it."

Thyra beamed from ear to ear under her new cap, quickly prancing up to Jonathan's side. "Well, if you're buying!"

Once he had finished paying, they went back outside into the main area. The crowd had thickened as more people and gryphons poured through the gates. Johnathen pulled the tickets out of his pocket and checked the seat numbers, consulting a very large map at the center of the circle.

"Looks like we have quite a ways to go," Johnathen stated, pointing at the area where the seats where. It was on the opposite side of the stadium, but they had plenty of time to get there.

The couple made their way around the large stadium before climbing multiple staircases to get to their section. There were hundreds of people wandering around, making their way towards their seats or grabbing a snack in preparation for the game. People parted out of the way for the large gryphoness as she walked through the crowd, puffing up proudly seeing how many Kites fans there were at the game.

Suddenly, the whole stadium thundered with the sound of thousands of fans shouting in excitement.

Thyra's hackle feathers pricked up and she started to bounce on her foreclaws. "Johnathen! I think it's starting!" she exclaimed, frantically looking at the seat section numbers posted above the entrance corridors.

"Come on! Hurry up!" she ran ahead and was soon lengths away from Jonathan. Being on all fours had its fair share of advantages as well as disadvantages but running was one of her strong suits. "Five O one. Five O five. Five ten!"

Thyra quickly bounded inside the corridor that led to the inner dome of the stadium. She gasped, getting her first sight of the playing field from high up above. It was colossal. Everybody was standing and cheering as the players ran onto the field. Music was being played by a large marching band near the field and an announcer called out each player as they ran out onto the field. It was a lot to take in all at once.

Johnathen approached from behind, a bit out of breath from having to run to catch up with his wife. He checked the tickets and motioned her towards their seats. One of the fold-down seats was much larger, looking like it was made for a couple but also doubled for gryphon seating.

Johnathen had to shout at Thyra in order for her to hear him. "I'll be right back!"

She nodded and turned her attention to the field, focusing on the Kites' players running onto the field. Her beak was agape in excitement and she could not keep still, shifting weight from one foreclaw to the other as she sat on the fold down seat. Her sharp avian eyes were able to focus on each player's face.

She knew them from all the games she had watched over the years. There were many different species of gryphons that played for the Jacksonville Kites, all sporting different colors of plumage. Many of them were a soft almond brown like she was, but there were a couple of lighter-colored kites and some much darker falcons.

Johnathen plopped down in his seat just as the announcer started to name off the players of the Atlanta Ospreys. Johnathen nudged into her wing shoulder with his elbow, holding a large plastic cup of golden beer out for her. She happily took it in her claws and brought it to her beak, taking a big gulp from the cup. Johnathen laughed, which made Thyra look at him, cocking her head inquisitively.

"What's so funny?!" she asked, curious what was funny about the players running onto the field.

"Your beak." He pointed at the large amount of foam that had gathered on the front of her beak, looking very much like she was sporting a new mustache.

All at once, the music stopped and everybody stood. Johnathen and Thyra quickly stood with the fans. She had to put her foreclaws on the seat in front of her to be able to see over the row of people. They all sang the national anthem together in unison, making the stadium shake with the booming voices of thousands of fans. After the quick ceremony, the band came back to life, and all the players started to take their positions. It was game time.

Chapter 8 The Gathering

A priest garbed in black slowly closed a large oak door behind him. He faced an elderly bishop who was sitting at a dark red desk, decorated by old relics and dusty tomes. All around the spacious room was an ample amount of bookshelves, filled with weather-beaten books. The only light source came from a stained glass window.

Bishop Matthew Darnwall was dressed in a white robe, accompanied by a long white and red sash. His semi-wrinkled face had a continuous furrowed brow, and he had no hair on his head. He did not look up at the visitor in black, but kept his eyes cast down on paperwork in front of him as he absently gestured, giving permission for the figure to approach.

"I have great news for you, Bishop," the figure in black said in a soft tone, slowly approaching the desk.

Matthew motioned for the man to sit, to which he quickly obeyed. He then looked up from his work and put down the pen, giving the priest his full attention. "I am listening."

"There is a member of our Gathering, George Armando, who has recently had an encounter with Johnathen Arkwright and that gryphon of his," the priest began.

The bishop's eyes widened in interest. "Go on."

"It seems that Johnathen and Brother Armando had a confrontation last night, which ended in Johnathen assaulting him," the priest continued.

A smile grew across the white-clothed, bald-headed man's face. It was not the fact that their parishioner had been struck that brought the bishop satisfaction, but the identity of the person who had assaulted him. "That is good news indeed, my son. Please, give my condolences to Brother Armando."

The priest nodded with a smile of his own, acknowledging the bishop's request.

"Also, be sure to tell Brother Armando that the church will be handling his legal matters in this case." The smile across his pale-skinned face grew even wider, thinking of the opportunity that he now had. "That will be all."

With the dismissal, the priest slowly stood up, and bowed. "Thank you. I will carry out your wish, Bishop."

Matthew gave the priest a nod before watching him exit the office. He leaned back in the sizable black leather chair and chuckled, his mood increasing considerably. This was no longer just another dull day, but one of action and plotting.

"Sundays sermon can wait," Mathew said aloud as he thought back to Johnathen's outburst in the middle of a similar sermon long ago. It still angered him. From time-to-time parishioners left The Gathering due to personal reasons, but none had been excommunicated like Johnathen had.

Matthew grew bitter, thinking back to that time years ago when Johnathen was a teenager and still a member of the Gathering. Matthew had only called himself a priest at the time, and Johnathen had been very involved with the Gathering. In fact, he had been studying to become a deacon.

For years, Johnathen had devoted himself to his studies and to the Gathering, but then something changed. He started to fall away, distancing himself from Matthew and the Gathering itself. Mathew had suspected it was because of Johnathen's relationship with that gryphoness, but that wasn't the sole reason. In reality, Johnathen had learned what Matthew was doing with the Gathering's money and the truths about what they were teaching.

The priest had been using the donations for his own financial gain, using it to buy multiple properties, exclusive investments, and paying high-ranking officials to look the other way. Johnathen had been disgusted by what Matthew was doing, but in Matthew's mind it was his own hard-earned money from the congregation. He was free to use it as he pleased, and if others saw it as corruption, they were fools. Matthew had a vision of a perfect world, and some 'laws' prevented him from accomplishing some goals, but with enough money, even the officers could be bought.

In the beginning, Matthew's Gathering had been small. He had created a new religion that was loosely based off of Catholicism, but with a flair for dramatic speaking that was so accepted in the Bible Belt. He quickly became quite popular in the small southern town. He had plucked his teachings from various religions. Most of them were average beliefs, while others were more extreme, like his teachings of white superiority. He was crafty about fostering those particular teachings, never coming right out and saying them as not to gather unwanted attention from the outside. Better to sow seeds into fertile minds.

The Gathering was, in a way, brainwashing the congregation, causing the people to make irrational decisions. Years of these sermons had led to complete obedience from the people and now they were Matthew's personal puppets for his debauchery.

After his excommunication, Johnathen had tried to warn others about Matthew and what he was trying to accomplish. Few would listen to him, and some quickly turned on Johnathen, cursing him for such accusations.

As time went by, their back and forth fights became

more brutal. Matthew attacked Johnathen within the church and politically, trying to outlaw marriage between humans and gryphons. It had resulted in a long political battle, but in the end, Johnathen and Keith came out the victors.

After losing at the polls, Matthew continued to attack Johnathen and Thyra from within the Gathering, sending members of the congregation to harass the couple. This had been successful for many years, but Johnathen fought back with multiple restraining orders and other legalities that prevented the constant abuse. In the end, Johnathen had won.

Matthew's defeat had left him feeling hollow and bitter, but now the fire was re-lit. Johnathen had screwed up and Mathew had the ammunition he needed to finally bury the man and his disgusting beast of a wife.

His lips twisted into a wicked smile. "I will show the people what comes of the immorality that those beasts can bring."

Chapter 9 The Kites VS the Ospreys

"Are you blind, ref?!" Thyra screeched in anger as a loud whistle echoed in the gargantuan stadium. The small amount of Kites fans cursed the referee along with her, shouting at him as he called a foul on the Kites.

Most of the stands were filled with Ospreys fans, as it was their home stadium. The score was tight, as was the tension of all the Kites fans. The Kites were down sixteen to eighteen and time was running out.

Thyra's brown-and-cream hackle feathers stood on end around her neck, showing her agitation. She reared and threw up one claw in disbelief and looked over at Johnathen, who was sitting calmly next to the disgruntled bird.

"Hey, he's only doing his job," Johnathen remarked, only trying to ruffle her feathers even more. Thyra's eyes narrowed at him, making her knifelike avian eyes even more frightening. Johnathen laughed, seeing that his needling had the desired effect.

"One job that he is doing quite poorly!" Thyra shouted back at him.

She had to shout. It was hard to hear each other with the thundering sounds of raucous fans and music playing. Johnathen sipped on his beer, turning back to watch the game as Thyra did the same, feathers slowly flattening out once more.

In the arena there were eight gryphons on the ground and four in the air. The Kites' blue and gold shone brightly in the bright stadium lighting as the white ball was being passed between them. The gryphon players were shouting and screeching at their fellow teammates as they frantically ran and flew around the field, trying anything to get open for the next pass.

Thyra's attention was on Tyler Smith. He was one of the largest gryphons on the field and had the broadest of wingspans. It was easy to pick him out from the rest of the smaller gryphons. She watched intently as Tyler tucked his wings in and fell like a boulder out of the sky, racing towards the ground.

Everybody in the stadium began to shout for him, having seen this maneuver before. It was the Kite's Hail Mary. The whole crowd stood to their feet, watching as Tyler rolled and flung open his wings at the last second, catching a great burst of speed. He soared low and pushed through two opposing gryphons, leaving him wide open for a pass. A team member on the ground passed the ball up to him. The white, egg-shaped oval flew through the air at great speed and was quickly caught in Tyler's strong foreclaws.

Everybody cheered even louder, watching as Tyler's wing beats became precise and powerful, trying to pick up more speed to get away from the other defense. Two gryphons on the ground leaped into the air, thrashing their smaller wings quickly to gain altitude and speed. Within moments, they had come within feet of Tyler, but it was already too late. With a quick spin, the large gryphon chucked the ball hard towards the goal. The egg-shaped ball barely missed the guardian gryphon's claws and soared into the goal.

The crowd around Thyra jumped to their feet, erupting with excitement. She placed talons on the seat in front of her to stand straight up, looking over the people. It was troublesome to continuously move about just to get a better view in the cramped stadium seating but worth it to see the game in person. The music grew louder, and the announcer yelled into the loudspeaker. Thyra screeched in glee, throwing her scaled forearms around Johnathen, laughing hysterically. The Osprey fans around the couple complained and shouted, hoping for some sort of foul or anything that would not make the goal count.

Tyler showed off for the crowd, gliding around close to the audience so that the wind from his wings rushed past the fans. He then screeched loudly in victory, performing somersaults and various air acrobatics.

The game wasn't quite finished yet, but the Ospreys returned to their side of the field, looking defeated as it was clear that time was running out. Johnathen looked up at the scoreboard. It changed from sixteen to nineteen for the Kites.

"I thought aerial scores were worth four points," he asked curiously, not quite understanding all the rules. Thyra was back in her seat, taking one last swig from her cup before putting it down on the ground.

"No-no, I thought you knew that! Aerial scores are worth three points. Ground throws are worth four."

"I always get those confused," he said.

"Well just remember that ground goals are more difficult to do, and that's why they are worth more," Thyra said with a bold grin, not even bothered by her husband's lack of knowledge. This game was done. There was no way the Ospreys could run it all the way to the opposite side and score within time.

The whistle blew loudly, and the ball was launched from an air-powered tube, sending it to the Ospreys side. The Kites sprinted towards the opposing team, four of them taking to the sky and assuming their positions. The gryphons collided with each other, taking their defensive positions as the Ospreys tried to get open.

One of the Kites lunged towards the Osprey player who possessed the ball and tackled him to the ground, but not before the player managed to pass it to his teammate. The opposite end of the stadium begun to cheer for their team, chanting and singing along while the Osprey player took to the sky with ball in his foreclaw, heading for the goal.

Their excitement was short lived as Tyler sped in from the side and rammed into the Osprey player. The player tumbled in mid-air, losing his balance and flaring his wings to keep from falling to the ground. A loud whistle blew again, signaling the end of the play.

Thyra clapped her claws together, applauding the Kites for their good defense. Many around her did the same.

The teams lined back up with the clock still running to make another play just as the timer ticked to zero. A bellowing horn shook the stadium, indicating the end of the game.

The Kites players leapt into the sky, shouting and screeching in triumph, while their fans exploded in excitement, jumping up and cheering loudly at their team's victory. It was a celebration that Thyra and Johnathen participated in happily. The players collided into each other, locking talons and slapping one another's wings together, proud of their win against the formidable Ospreys.

While the winning team's fans continued to celebrate, thousands of people and gryphons alike began to leave the stadium, pouring out of the exits towards the vast parking lot.

"What a game!" Thyra exclaimed, rising from her seat to follow a long line of people out towards the exit.

"It was pretty close. For a moment, I thought the Kites were going to lose," Johnathen replied, following closely behind his wife.

The line moved at a steady pace, trickling down the

stairs and out into the midway. The once bustling food vendors were now preparing to shut down, making their last sales of the season.

"Well I never lost hope," Thyra said proudly, hanging back in the line to walk next to Johnathen as the fans continued to spread out, moving towards the main gates much like water flowing down a steep river.

A foreign, high-pitched voice came from beside Thyra and Johnathen, "Neither did I. Tyler Smith always performs the best under pressure."

They turned to face the origin of the voice. A brightly-colored violet gryphoness moved alongside Thyra, sporting the same Kites hat that Thyra wore. This new gryphoness appeared to be bubbly and happy, either from the win, her personality, or the amount of alcohol she had imbibed.

She looked at Thyra, her satin black beak gleaming bright in a friendly grin. Thyra returned the smile, happy to speak with another gryphon, especially one that was a fan of her favorite team.

Thyra had never seen another gryphon with this striking coloration and accent before. Her feathers shifted in color from dark blue to shimmering violet depending on the way the light hit them. Her black beak was narrow and straight, which showed her amused expression even more so than the curved hook beak of a raptor. A long, cream-colored feline tail slowly twitched behind her.

"I know, right? He always puts out when the going gets rough," Thyra replied, looking into the gryphoness' deep blue eyes.

"I'm sure he puts out for more than just the game!" the gryphoness joked and begun to laugh, making Thyra do the same. Johnathen forced a smile as he walked beside the two gryphonesses. The turn in their conversation was making him feel a little awkward.

"I...I will be right back Thyra. Going to go use the bathroom." Johnathen quickly said.

Thyra nodded to Johnathen as he wandered off through the crowd towards the restrooms. The violet gryphoness looked inquisitive for a minute. She watched Johnathen leave, and then looked down at Thyra's claws, spotting the ring on her finger.

"Oh shit! I'm sorry about that. Totally didn't know you were with him, or I wouldn't have made that comment," she explained, still beaming from ear to ear.

Thyra looked over her shoulder, watching Johnathen disappear into the sea of people.

"It's alright. Not many would think that we are together."

The brightly colored gryphoness nodded, sitting back on her haunches in front of Thyra. People made a point to walk around the two gryphonesses sitting in the middle of the corridor, not wanting to bump into the pair. "It's not exactly a traditional relationship, especially for this part of the country. I bet you all are the first southern gryphon and human pair."

Thyra perked an eye ridge. "How exactly did you know I'm from around here?"

"It's a dead giveaway, really. Your coloration is constant with the resident red tail, and if that wasn't enough, the accent was obvious the moment you opened your beak," the gryphoness answered back, being quite forward.

"Fair enough. Well, since we are on that subject, your coloration is new to me. Where exactly are you from?" Thyra asked. She was not an uneducated bird by any means. In fact, she was proud of the fact that she knew many different species of gryphon and their origin. It bothered her that she could not guess what species this gryphoness belonged to.

"If you must know, I'm originally from Africa, but lived most of my life in Spain," the gryphoness said with pride, puffing up her white chest feathers. "You can call me Isabell."

Thyra smiled to her, touching her forehead to the smaller bird's forehead in the traditional form of greeting. "I'm Thyra. Nice to meet another gryphon Kites fan!"

Johnathen came up from behind the two hens, surprised to find them conversing with one another as if they were long lost friends. "Seems you made a new friend, hun."

Thyra turned to look at Johnathen with a pleased chirp before nodding in response. "Yeah! She's a pretty cool bird."

The three of them began to walk towards the exit once again. By now the crowd was thinning out, which made it much easier for them to walk side-by-side.

"I don't like to brag, but I am a pretty cool bird. Actually, I love to brag," Isabell said and purred deep in her chest, amused with herself. "My name is Isabell."

"Oh, and this is my husband, Johnathen," Thyra said and Johnathen waved a hello as they walked.

Isabell grinned up at him. "Well you caught yourself a looker, that's for sure," she said in her version of flattery.

Johnathen was a bit shocked at the flirty comment but took it as a compliment since she was foreign. He wondered why Isabel was alone, but felt it was rude to ask.

"I got pretty lucky," Thyra beamed, looking up at Johnathen.

He threw his arm around Thyra's neck as they walked together, holding her close. "No, I'm the one that hit the lottery."

"Enough. You all are going to make me sick," Isabell cut in, making a fake gagging sound.

Thyra and Johnathen laughed and the three of them

made their way through the front gates of the stadium into the vast parking lot.

"Where do you live?" Johnathen asked, wondering how far she had flown for the game.

"Not too far, a little town called Perry. A little less than an hour from here by wing."

Thyra's long eartufts perked up, she had visited the town a couple times in the past. "Perry? That's only a half hour by wing from Macon!"

Isabell's small, rounded ears flicked in excitement at the good news and she reached for a pouch hanging from her side. "Then I am definitely going to need your phone number."

Isabell drew out a rather large cell phone from the leather satchel and handed it over to Thyra. She took the phone in both foreclaws, amused by the decorations of purple glitter and other little trinkets.

Thyra typed in the numbers and handed it back with a smile. "I'll look forward to hanging out with you soon!"

"We will have to get together for the next game," Isabell replied. "I know a great sports bar between Macon and Perry that shows all the gryphon league games."

The party approached Johnathen's station wagon and said their goodbyes. Johnathen shook Isabell's foreclaw and Thyra gave her one more beak nudge before the gryphoness turned and took to the air with light wing beats, her feathers shifting in brilliant colors in the bright sunlight as she quickly gained altitude.

"Well that was a pleasant surprise," Thyra said quite happily, hopping into the passenger seat.

"Always good to make new friends, especially another gryphon," he agreed.

Johnathen closed the door behind her and made his

way into the driver's seat. He started the engine and pulled into the slow line of cars leaving the extensive parking lot. Once finally free of the traffic, he shifted into a new gear, gaining speed as he pulled onto a main road. The sun was setting behind the stadium, making the goliath structure glow a rusty orange as it slowly disappeared into the horizon.

"I still can't get over it. We have lived in Macon for years and I have yet to find another local gryphoness," Thyra said in an excited tone.

"Hopefully Isabell will work out for you. Maybe you can cluck around with her instead of me all the time. My ears could use a break," he teased.

"You don't make for a very good conversation hen anyways." Thyra snorted in reply.

Chapter 10 Calm Before The Storm

Johnathen's hand shot out from under the covers, slapping the alarm's snooze button from complete muscle memory. But the loud beeping didn't stop. He drew the sheets off of his face and reached for his cell phone where it sat, buzzing and beeping on the night stand. Thyra groaned in protest at the sound, ruffling and rolling over in bed next to him.

Johnathen's eyes squinted as he tried to read his phone, vision still blurry in his groggy morning state. It was a text from Keith.

Turn on the Macon morning news.

He was confused as to why Keith would text him something like that, but it had to be important. Johnathen reached over, grabbed the remote, and turned on the thin flat screen attached to the wall.

Thyra turned over in bed and huffed deeply, clearly aggravated by the entire disturbance. She opened her eyes slightly, staring at Johnathen with irritation.

"W...what are you doing?" she said, yawning in a low, dazed voice.

Johnathen was busy flipping through the channels, the bright white light filling the room in the early morning making him squint. "Keith told me to turn on the news."

Thyra wasn't interested. She pulled the covers over her head, trying to hide from the light.

Johnathen came across the main news channel and grew wide-eyed as he instantly recognized the man that was being interviewed. It was the old man from the restaurant who Johnathen had punched. He had a large bandage that covered most of his fat nose, and a black eye. For some reason, he was also wearing a sling for his right arm.

"*I tried to be civil with the young'n'. I politely asked him and his wife to quiet down. She was one of them gryphons and did she have a temper! She yelled at me, then he stood up and struck me right in the face.*"

Fury welled within Johnathen as he watched the old man blatantly lie to the interviewer. Thyra was now peeking her head out from under the blanket, staring in disbelief at the television. At the bottom of the screen, it had the man's name, George Armando.

Just then, Johnathen's phone began to ring and he quickly answered it. "Yeah, I see it Keith. No. I didn't know he'd be interviewed on the morning news."

Thyra watched the television while Johnathen talked to his friend. George continued to bash her husband and herself, calling them menaces to the town and a danger to the community. Her eyes grew wide as Matthew, the bishop of The Gathering, suddenly appeared next to George.

Thyra wrapped her talons around Johnathen's arm, tugging it to get his attention. Johnathen fell silent on seeing Matthew on the screen, his blood boiling.

"*We simply cannot have these ungodly people in our community. There must be repercussions for Mr. Arkwright's actions, not only to George but to God as well. His 'wife' is a danger to us all. She is an abomination before the Lord's eyes. They walk the sinner's path and will bring destruction to our good faith. Leviticus twenty tells us . . ."*

The remote hit the wall with a loud crack. The flimsy plastic shattered into pieces and the television turned off, leaving the room almost completely black, apart from the little slivers of yellow light from the edges of the curtains. All was silent for several moments.

Johnathen's hands were clenched into fists, and he shook with anger. Thyra moved in closer to him and pressed herself against her husband, letting out a gentle thrum. Slowly the tension within him began to ease and he wrapped an arm around her neck and pulled her closer.

"Don't let that asshole get to you," she said gently. "He's only trying to provoke you."

"I know he is, and it's working," Johnathen replied.

He let go of her and threw off the covers to sit on the edge of the bed. He placed his phone on the nightstand and looked at the digital clock. It was almost time for the alarm to go off, so Johnathen switched it off and stood up, then walked into the bathroom to start his morning routine.

The edges of Thyra's beak curved down in an avian version of a frown. She felt terrible for Johnathen. She had watched him go through so much for her and it was times like this that made her think his life would be so much easier without her. For a moment Thyra hated herself, hated that she was different from everyone else. She despised the people in this town and detested The Gathering for casting such strong judgments on gryphons. Sometimes she wished they could just move far away and never have to return to this city.

She shook her feathered head. No. This was their home. They had been through this once before and won. This time would be no different.

With newfound energy, Thyra hopped off of the bed. She stretched out, her foreclaws way out in front, her rear end raised in the air. She opened her long wings as much as she could in the room without knocking anything over. Then Thyra stood back up, tucked her wings in, and made her way over to the closet to pick out Johnathen's clothes for the day.

Thyra's phone vibrated and jumped across the nightstand. Her long eartufts perked and flicked at the sudden noise and she reached over to grab the bulky old phone.

It was a message from Keith. *Is Johnathen ok?*

She sat down on her haunches, holding the phone with both sets of talons. *Yeah, just a little shook up and pissed off.*

While she waited for his reply, Thyra went to the news channel's website and looked up as much information she could about the interview.

Another text from Keith came through. *I figured as much after seeing that douchebag bishop slamming y'all.*

Thyra carried the cell phone into the living room and hopped up onto the spacious brown leather couch, making herself comfortable while she texted her reply. *It wasn't good. This is not going to go well, is it?*

The gryphoness grabbed the remote and turned on the living room TV. She began flipping through the local channels and every local morning news report had Johnathen's face at the bottom of the screen while commentators babbled on about that night's happenings.

She could understand why the incident would make local news, this being a small town, but she'd had no idea it would be blown so much out of proportion. Her eartufts flicked as she heard the shower cut off and the hairdryer kick on. The phone vibrated with another new message from Keith.

No. It's not good at all. There is already someone here looking for him at the office.

"Skies!" Thyra cursed under her breath.

Thyra heard the hairdryer turn off. She quickly picked up the remote and switched to her morning talk show as Johnathen made his way into the living room. He threw on his white dress shirt and poured himself a bowl of cereal, silently lost in his own thoughts. Thyra watched him out of the corner of her eye as he tapped on the digital tablet mounted to the kitchen bar table. His brow furrowed more, clearly agitated by what he was reading.

She crawled off of the couch and made her way over to him, claws clicking against the dark hardwood floor. Johnathen turned to look over at her as she sat on her haunches and used her foreclaws to begin fastening his shirt's buttons.

"We can take care of this mess, together. It will just take time is all," Thyra promised him while she worked the last button into place.

He frowned but nodded in response. A loud ringtone broke the silence between them. Johnathen reached into his pocket and answered the call.

"Keith? Yes. I saw it all. What? Ok. Thanks for the heads up." Johnathen sighed exhaustedly and hung up.

"What did Keith say?" Thyra wondered, watching as Johnathen stood up from the barstool to grab his black suit jacket.

"There's a process server at work already," he replied, putting on his jacket and grabbing the car keys.

"That was quick. I would think that it would take several days to put together a summons." Thyra was no stranger to how the laws worked. She had been in the courtroom herself many times and visited Johnathen on some of his cases.

"Usually it does, but I'm not too surprised at how quickly it came. Mathew has a lot of contacts on his payroll." He grabbed the briefcase off of the dining room table before stopping and leaning down to give Thyra a quick kiss on the beak.

"Be careful," she said in a worried tone, watching as he made his way out the door and into the garage.

Thyra walked back over to the couch to slump onto it once again, her brown-and-cream feathers laid flat against her body in distress. She tried to calm herself as the idle chatting from the people on television droned on. The moment didn't last long as her cell phone interrupted her once again. This time it was a message from Jimmie, her boss.

Ten orders today. Get here ASAP.

Thyra groaned and tossed the phone on the coffee table before rolling over on her back. She watched the ceiling fan spin, high up on the vaulted ceiling of her home, gathering her thoughts and finding the energy to get up. She did not have time for coffee, or her other morning routines.

Thyra rolled off the couch and walked over to a large kitchen window, looking up at the clear skies. "Well at least the weather is nice today."

&♥

Thunder cracked loudly in the air, streaks of light blinding Thyra's eyes as she flew low to the ground, cursing under her breath. Wind whipped her feathers in all directions, her wings beating hard against the powerful gusts to keep altitude. She squinted, trying to keep the rain out of her eyes as much as possible.

Another flash of glaring light filled the dark sky,

showing the outline of the large pavilion below. Thyra tucked her wings and fell quickly, angling her red tail feathers downward, aiming towards the entrance. She flared her wings open and landed with a loud *thud* just under the pavilion's roof. The farmers market was mostly empty that day, which made the spacious pavilion area seem even bigger than normal. Many vendors had stayed home after checking the weather, something that Thyra wished she had done earlier.

Her feathers were disheveled and shaggy, dripping from being completely saturated. A light rain would bead off the natural oils in her feathers, but in a heavy downpour it did not matter. She walked through the small crowd of people who stared with blank expressions at the appearance of the drenched and agitated gryphoness. She clearly looked unhappy as the soaked leather of her satchels creaked with every step.

Jimmie looked up to see the saturated gryphoness and could not help but flash an amused grin. He was wearing a bright yellow rain coat to keep himself as dry as possible during the trips to the truck.

"Well this weather came outta nowhere," he said.

Thyra gave the old white haired man a dull look. "No shit."

She shook her feathers, much like a canine would do after a bath. Water flung in every direction, some of it hitting Jimmie's raincoat. Thyra sat down in front of the vegetable stand, trying to fluff up her wet feathers while shivering.

Jimmie grabbed a large towel he had tucked away in a crate and handed it over to Thyra. She gratefully took it in her foreclaws and began to rub it through her soaked plumage.

"Well, things started out great, but I don't reckon you'll be running many more deliveries today if the weather don't turn better," Jimmie observed, looking regretfully at the counter. He had already pulled out the orders Thyra needed to deliver and had them sitting out in brown bags.

Thyra was busy drying herself as much as possible, but nodded in response. She looked more like a giant feather duster that fell into a sink than an actual gryphon. "It was hard enough to get here, much less fly with extra weight."

She opened her wings, checking the bent primaries and secondaries. The wind had really done a number on them and it would take some preening to get them back in order.

"Just going to be one of those days, I guess," Thyra said, clearly exhausted from the flight.

Lightning danced across the sky again, thunder boomed in the distance as Thyra wrapped the towel around her shoulders, shivering from the cold. Jimmie reached over to his propane heater, turning it up a bit and sat down on a crate next to it. Thyra walked around the stand to lie on the concrete floor directly in front of the furnace, letting out a pleased trill as the warmth did wonders for her body.

"It ain't off to a good start, I guess. What with the weather and what's going on with Johnathen," the man said.

She perked her eartufts at the mention of Johnathen's name. She avoided eye contact, instead turning her head to watch the flames dance across the metal surface of the heater. "You saw all that on the news already, Jimmie?"

"I always watch the news in the mornin'. Gotta see what's going on in town," Jimmie stated, picking up a weathered old mug and taking a sip.

Thyra let out a sigh, moving around a little bit to angle her damp parts towards the heat. "I really wish this wouldn't have gone public like it did."

She continued to stare into the flames, watching them lick and flicker gently. Jimmie busied himself sorting out his vegetables and fruits, taking count of his stock. The sound of the rain pouring hard against the large metal roof of the spacious pavilion caused her to drift into unconsciousness.

Jimmie looked down at the now sleeping gryphon and took another dry blanket out from one of the crates. He shook it off and draped it across her back, trying to keep her warm. Usually he wouldn't have let Thyra just fall asleep like that, but she was stuck on the ground until the storm lightened up. A customer caught his attention, and he left Thyra fast asleep.

ᵴ🖈

Johnathen arrived at work and leaned back in the seat of his car, letting out a heavy sigh. He looked at himself in the rear view mirror as heavy rain battered down on the roof.

I should just call out, he thought. Johnathen was not looking forward to what awaited him at the office, and the rain was not helping. *I hope Thyra didn't go to work today. She'd probably be soaking wet by now.*

Thinking about his wife struggling to fly in strong winds and heavy rain always worried him. She was an excellent flier, but was so small in an open and wild sky. Even the largest species of gryphon could injure one of their wings or become overpowered by an overly strong wind and fall to their deaths.

Johnathen closed his eyes, trying to get the awful thoughts out of his head. It took all his mental strength to take the car keys out of the ignition and grab his umbrella before throwing open the door. Lightning danced across the gray sky as the downpour opened up further, whisking rain left and right.

He hurriedly opened up his umbrella, seeking shelter underneath it while the wind picked up, threatening to tear the fabric in two. He closed the car door and walked briskly across the parking lot, now just a huge puddle from the heavy downpour. Johnathen grumbled as he felt the cold water seeping into his brown leather shoes and soaking his socks.

A large gust of wind whipped down suddenly, tearing the small umbrella from his hand. He cursed loudly while it flew across the lot and out of sight, leaving him exposed to the elements. By the time Johnathen stepped into the large lobby, he was soaked.

His dark hair lay in many different directions, dripping from the heavy rain. Every step with his soaked leather shoes caused a loud squeak while he bounded towards the elevator.

The usually-bubbly receptionist who sat behind the granite counter was silent, trying not to make eye contact as he stood quietly, waiting for the elevator to come down. Johnathen glanced over at her, unable to manage a fake smile or wave hello. Instead, he stared down at the white tile as rainwater pooled around his feet.

The elevator dinged, and the doors opened slowly. Johnathen walked to the corner of the small lift and rested against it. He breathed deeply, trying to mentally prepare himself as best as he could as he ascended to the floor where his personal hell awaited. Way too quickly, the elevator stopped and the doors opened.

The floor went quiet as people stopped talking and turned to look at him. He strode towards his office and heads popped over the many cubicles to catch a glimpse of him walking by. Just before he stepped inside, he saw a couple of figures standing in the conference room on the far end of the floor.

"John," said a familiar voice from behind him. Keith kept his voice low and calm, hating to be the bearer of bad news. "They're in there, waiting for you."

Johnathen put down his dripping briefcase and hung

his coat up on the rack, then turned to face a mirror hanging up on the other side of the office. His black suit was drenched, and his hair was a complete mess. He was in no shape to present himself in front of his boss or the representatives of the prosecution.

"Who all is in there?" Johnathen asked as he made his way over to his desk.

"It looks like some boys from the Kennedy group," Keith replied. "Dean's with them."

Johnathen picked up a comb from one of his drawers and started to brush his hair back, making it at least somewhat presentable. Dean was Johnathen and Keith's boss and the CEO of their firm. A meeting involving Dean was usually never good, but this was going to be a catastrophe.

"I expected as much," Johnathen replied, keeping his voice cool and collected but internally, he was terrified. Being served with a lawsuit was nothing he could not handle, but the nature of the charges could reflect badly on the firm. There were many punishments his boss could dish out, and they ranged from a slap on the wrist to being fired.

Johnathen straightened up his gray paisley tie, took one last look in the mirror and walked towards the door. Keith reached out and placed his hand on Johnathen's shoulder, stopping him for a second.

"Hey, bud. Whatever happens I'm here for you," he said.

Johnathen patted him on the shoulder and walked on by. "Thanks."

Chapter 11 Dreams

Thyra's wings beat one last time in a hard backstroke before she landed roughly onto the muddy ground. She frowned as her talons sank deep into the brown sludge. The smell of damp earth filled her nares as she pulled her talons free and her made way to the driveway.

The once bellowing storm had lessened to a sprinkle just as she was getting off of work. Nevertheless, Thyra was soaked to the bone and her wings were tired and sore from flying in the rain all day long. Her muscles cried out as she folded her wings away, tucking them close to her side.

"I can't wait to take a nice warm shower," she said to herself as she stood in front of the garage door.

The thought of warm water heating her sore muscles and easing her aching joints brought a smile on her yellow-tinted beak. She sat on her haunches and used her dexterous foreclaws to unlatch the front leather pocket of her harness, digging around for the clicker. She pushed the button on the device but to her surprise, nothing happened. Thyra looked at the closed garage door curiously and then tried it again.

Still nothing.

Thyra huffed through her nares in agitation and made her way around the house to the front door. Once under the cover of the front porch, she shook herself off, spreading her wings and violently shaking water in every direction.

Her damp brown and cream feathers stood on end as she fumbled around in the same pouch once again for her keys. She struggled to grip the jingling things. They were difficult to manipulate with her large claws. She could never understand why with all this technology humans still used these tiny, frustrating, metal objects to lock things up. Thyra cursed under her breath, dropping them several times while attempting to unlock the door, but finally she was inside.

The house was dark and cold, alerting Thyra that there was something wrong. She reached over to flip on the hallway light switch, but nothing happened.

"Skies, looks like the power is out," she said exhaustedly, sick of this entire day.

Her drenched feathers dripped water all over the clean hardwood floor, and the mud from her claws left a trail down the hallway into the kitchen. She would have to worry about cleaning all that up later, but there was only one thought on her mind right now, that shower.

She unlatched the main satchel on the front side of the harness and threw it on the granite kitchen countertop. The keys and her cellphone clanked around together inside the satchel as it hit the stone surface. Then she worked her talons across the rest of the harness, unlatching the various buckles and clasps until it all fell onto the dark wooden floor.

She left the leather harness and satchels laying where they were and made her way into the bedroom. The blackout curtains on the windows made the room even darker than the rest of the house. The sound of rolling thunder could be heard in the distance, making the house vibrate with its deep bass.

She walked into the bathroom and grunted at the impenetrable darkness inside. Her eyes were great for seeing long distances in the daytime but were almost useless in low light. She couldn't even make out the showerhead in the back of the bathroom.

Thyra was determined to have that hot shower though. At that moment, it seemed like it would be the best thing to happen on this horrible day. The gryphoness went back into the bedroom, remembering the decorative scented candles on the dresser. She had picked them out years ago, and they had likely lost their scent. Might as well put them to their destined use.

Now if I were a lighter, where would I be? She tried to think about the last time she saw one. Johnathen had stopped smoking quite some time ago but would occasionally bum one from Keith on their guys' nights. Johnathen always thought he was so smooth with hiding the fact he would occasionally smoke from her, but she was wiser than he thought.

She made her way back into the kitchen, passing the puddle of water and spots of mud where she had taken off her harness. She padded down the dark hallway and into Johnathen's office.

This room was brighter than the others. Decorative curtains were pulled back from the large window to allow as much natural light into the area as possible. Framed pictures and other little trinkets adorned Johnathen's dark oak desk and the tall bookcases behind it were filled with law books.

A large vase on one side of his desk held an arrangement made from Thyra's own feathers, ranging from the maroon red of her tail feathers and the longer primaries of her wings. She made her way behind the desk, moving the black leather chair out of the way to open one of the drawers.

She fumbled through the papers and clutter inside to try to find the object she was seeking. The computer monitor on the desk shook back and forth while she did so. After searching the drawers, she sat down on her haunches and grumbled, trying to think where else he might have hidden that lighter.

Thyra's eyes settled on a little garnished wooden box, decorated with golden leaves that sat on one of the bookshelves. She grabbed it off the shelf and opened it up. Her eyes widened in surprise and a little grin flashed across her beak.

"Pay-dirt," she said with a shake of her head. The box was full of cigars with a matchbook lying on top. She took the matches out, placed the cigar box down on his desk, and padded back into the master bathroom. She would have been angrier about his sneaky habit if it wasn't so convenient at the moment.

She took one of the candles off of the dresser and brought it into the bathroom with her. At least it wasn't cigarettes. Thyra secretly liked the smell of cigars.

Thyra struggled with the small stick end of the match, holding it in her claws and trying to strike it against the rough patch on the side of the small box. These matches were definitely not made for a gryphon's cumbersome claws to handle.

It took her a few attempts, but finally she had the little match lit. She held it to the candle, watching as it took new life and filled the dark room with a rich, orange glow. The light danced and licked across the walls, reflecting brightly in the mirror and the glass surface of the shower. The candle's scent, which had seemed dead after years of disuse, was stoked to life by the heat of the flame.

Feeling much better about the situation, Thyra made her way over to the shower and turned it on, letting the water flow and heat up. The smell of clean, hot water began to fill the air, mixing with the vanilla candle scent to create a relaxing aroma.

Thyra opened the shower door and stepped inside, letting the hot water rush across her cold, damp feathers. Immediately, a sigh of relief escaped her beak as the hot water soaked into her down, making her shiver and stretch out inside the spacious shower. Her head buzzed pleasantly from the feeling, and for a moment, she completely forgot about her aching muscles.

She stretched out her wings in the shower as much as she could, letting the water bead across the primaries and secondaries. She reached for the soap and started to work it between her talons to cleanse them from the caked-up mud. The flickering candle provided just enough light for her to see where the dirt and grime was on her talons and wash it all away.

After a good long soak Thyra turned off the water, feeling revitalized. She looked at herself in the foggy bathroom mirror as the flames gleamed and reflected off of her beak. The gryphoness dried off with one of the towels, wincing as one of her main wing muscles ached in pain, rudely reminding her of her strenuous day.

Thyra let the towel drop to the floor once she was done with it and made her way into the main living room. The room was dark and dreary as the rain pattered against the windows. She eyed the dry bar in the corner of the room. The various glassware and bottles of liquor looked quite inviting to the beaten down gryphoness.

"This should do the trick."

The cork of the whisky bottle popped off easily. She grabbed one of the crystal glasses sitting on the shelf and placed it in front of her, then carefully poured the brown liquor until the glass was half full. She wrapped her large talons around the glass, making a clinking noise as she picked it up and held it beneath her beak.

The scent of the warm whisky filled her nares, making her hackle feathers stand up. Her beak opened slightly she tilted the glass back, letting it pour over her tongue. She swallowed the brown liquid and shivered, her feathers fluffing up as it burned down the back of her throat.

Thunder boomed once again, causing the glasses to

rattle against one another as the house shuddered gently. Thyra held the glass in her beak and made her way over to the window to look outside.

The rain was coming down hard once again, turning the streets into small rivers. She walked back to the brown couch in the middle of the room and placed the glass on the end table before hopping up on the soft cushions and tossing a blanket over herself.

The gryphoness purred with delight, relaxing in the warm confines of her favorite spot. Her talons wrapped tightly around the glass again and she took another deep gulp of the whisky, letting it slowly take its effect over her.

The gentle sound of pattering on the rooftop lulled Thyra into a calm state. She found her eyes getting heavier with every passing moment and every sip of the powerful elixir. Her mind began to wander, bringing back memories of her younger life.

Thyra was looking out of the large window of a very plain room, watching the rain pour down outside. It was almost pitch black outside, except for the tall street lamps that gave just enough light to see into the distance. There were red flowers on the window sill, bending in the strong gusts of wind.

Flashes of lightning blinded her for a second. She blinked and turned away from the window. The walls of the room were painted a pure white, and the floor was concrete. Two men dressed in white coats were in the room with her, talking amongst themselves.

One of the men turned to look at her. "Thyra."

She got up off her haunches and approached the desk they were sitting at. Her bright green eyes were instantly drawn to the metal rings tied together on the center of the table. She reached towards them with a foreclaw, picking the rings up and dangling them in the air.

"We would like to see you complete this puzzle."

She looked up at the two men, but her memory of their faces was blurry. In her younger years she had thought that most humans looked the same. She glanced at the rings and gave them a nod. She started to rotate the shining rings, pulling at them, squeezing them together, trying to separate them. It was a bit difficult to maneuver the metal pieces, but soon had the multiple pieces laid out on the table.

Thyra watched one man scribble onto a notepad while the other reached into his pocket to pull out a green and yellow pear. He held it out to her and her mouth watered instantly at seeing the juicy piece of fruit. Thyra reached out and gently took the pear from the man's hand, bringing it to her beak and taking a large chunk from it. She swallowed it down, the juices sending shivers up her spine as they ran across her pink avian tongue.

While the two men talked between themselves, more details of the room filtered into her memories. There was a large blackboard with elementary math problems written on it, a gryphon-sized cream-colored pillow, littered with her brown feathers, and a couple of small books upon a bookshelf. The sound of thunder filled her ears, making them flick in response as she swallowed down the last savory sweet bite of the pear.

One of the men looked down at his watch and nodded back to the other. "That's enough for today. Get some rest, Thyra."

It was the same man that had talked before; the only man who would talk to her for the longest time. Despite his blurry face, that voice was burned into her memory like a record on repeat. Both of them stood up from the table and made their way out through the door in the far back of the room. She sat silently and watched them make their exit, then shut the door and locked it behind them

Everything blurred. The images of the white room faded away slowly as the sound of footsteps roused Thyra from her memories. Her eyes opened just as the door handle clicked. She sat on the couch, watching the door as it slowly opened in the hallway. A figure quickly entered and shut the door behind itself and Thyra strained her eyes to see.

Johnathen's voice boomed in the silent and dark house. "Thyra? You home?"

Thyra quickly let out a sigh of relief, "Yeah, I'm in the living room." A bright white light beamed down the hallway, reflecting off the granite countertops as it filled the living room with a dull luminescence.

"Having a little nap? Seems like you're always napping." Johnathen stated.

"Well, guess it's just the feline in me," she replied.

Johnathen placed his keys and light on the island table. He leaned down to take off his shoes, noticing the soaked leather harness lying in a heap next to him. "Yeah, looks like the damned power is out," he said, but clearly he was irritated by more than just the power outage.

"No, it's not, I just like sitting completely in the dark with nothing to do but drink." she said with a chuckle, trying to lighten his mood.

Johnathen made his way into the living room, his eyes adjusting to the darkness. He could make out the shape of his wife sprawled along the full length of her favorite couch. She smiled as she lifted the empty crystal glass.

"You want another?" He asked jokingly, already knowing the answer to that question.

"Naturally," she purred.

The Gryphon Generation

Johnathen grabbed the glass out of her foreclaws and made his way over to the wet bar. He set the glasses down on the table and popped off the cork from the whisky bottle.

"So, how was your day?" he asked as he poured her another drink. The sound of thunder echoed again, this time far in the distance, and she noticed that the rain had started to die down.

She motioned towards the windows with a foretalon. "Awful. It's not exactly the ideal flying weather."

"I'll bet. Flying in that rain can't have been much fun. It sure as hell sucked to drive in it."

Johnathen poured himself a drink of the same brown liquor before putting the bottle away. Thyra sat up, opening her beak in another loud yawn as she made room for Johnathen on the couch. He made his way over with both glasses and handed one to Thyra.

"How did it go at the office?" Thyra asked, her tone a bit more serious.

Johnathen swirled the glass a little before tilting it back and taking a big gulp of the whisky, letting it burn the back of his throat before responding. "About as expected. I've been suspended."

Thyra leaned in against him, rubbing her smooth beak into his neck, while wrapping a long wing around him. He was soaking wet and quite cold to the touch, which made her feathers rouse. "What does that actually mean? For us? How bad is it?"

Johnathen sat back on the couch, his eyes slowly adjusting to the dim light of the room. The candle flickered back and forth on the coffee table, causing the crystal of the glass to shine. "Not only will I not be allowed back into the office to practice law until this all blows over, but all my current clients have been handed over to other lawyers, for the time being. In other words, it's essentially a pay cut. A pretty big one."

Thyra sat silently and listened, bringing her glass to her beak once again to take another gulp. She didn't know what to say, nor what to do.

"Also, it means my reputation is tarnished." Johnathen sighed and placed the empty glass down on the coffee table. He brought his hands up to rub his eyes, exhausted both mentally and physically. "After all I have done, and how far I have advanced in the company. I don't-."

"Johnathen." Thyra interrupted. She sat on her haunches next to him and wrapped a wing tight around his body. Johnathen stared into her strong green avian eyes and she leaned in to rub her feathery cheek up against his and said softly in his ear, "We will be alright. Just get through this, and it will all be over."

Johnathen leaned back into her, letting her radiating warmth and soft feathers ease his mind for a minute. "This thing with Matthew. It will be a long, hard battle, just as before."

"And I will be with you every step of the way," she promised.

They pressed foreheads together, enjoying the moment before Johnathen stood up. Thyra smiled to him and resumed her lazy position on the now completely free couch once again.

"If you don't mind, I need a cigar," he announced.

Thyra frowned at him, and clicked her beak, ear tufts pinned back in slight irritation. She huffed and turned her head to look away, acting more upset than she was. "Well, you did have a bad day. As long as it's a cigar and not a cigarette, then fine . . . I guess."

Chapter 12 Idle Hands

The morning sunlight reflected off the granite countertops, and the smell of fresh brewed coffee was heavy in the air. Thyra reached for the pot and poured herself a cup then dropped down to all fours, carrying the coffee cup in her beak.

The digital clock on the kitchen counter was still blinking twelve o'clock after yesterday's power outage. Thyra reminded herself to set it as she made her way down the hallway next to the living room. She passed Johnathen's office and opened the patio door that led out onto the upstairs balcony where she did most of her morning decompression. The smell of moist earth and fresh rain filled her lungs in the cool summer morning. Water quickly began to bead off of her feathers from the humidity in the southern air while she lay down on an outdoor mesh lounge.

She took a sip of the hot black coffee and watched as the neighbors bustled about, grabbing the morning paper, tending to their gardens, and mowing their lawns before it became too hot. Thyra pulled out her phone from the small pouch she always wore around her neck and began to scroll through the news, occasionally sipping the bold coffee as she read about what was going on in the world.

"Nothing about Johnathen," she said, grateful for the reprieve.

The sounds of a large vehicle's brakes caused Thyra to look down. A long yellow school bus had pulled up to the corner. Kids ran out of their houses, laughing and carrying on. One child looked up at her and waved hello. She grinned back and waved back with a foreclaw, watching as they all boarded before the bus drove away.

Her ear tufts stood in attention as the door behind her creaked open. She looked back at Johnathen as he stumbled onto the patio, holding a mug in his left hand. He wore nothing but green pajama pants, which caused Thyra's eye ridge to raise in question.

"Mornin', hun. You think you should put on a shirt so you don't scare the neighbors?" Thyra said gently, amused at his disheveled appearance.

Johnathen had stayed up most of the night sitting on the covered back porch and had come to bed reeking of liquor and cigar smoke. His eyes were bloodshot, and his hair looked like a pile of shaved dog fur. He squinted in the early light and took a sip of coffee, grumbling a slight response to her.

Thyra thought it best to leave him be. They sat silently, drinking their morning joe and browsing through their phones until the sun was well above the horizon.

Thyra's phone dinged and vibrated in her foreclaw. She read the message then put down her phone and coffee cup. Yawning, she reached forward as far as she could and raised her rump into the air, stretching out her back much like a feline would.

"Was that Jimmie?" Johnathen asked, leaning back to dodge her wing while she stretched.

"Yeah, lots of deliveries today. Especially after yesterday's storm slowed me down."

Johnathen nodded and took another sip as Thyra gathered her things and made her way to the balcony door.

"I hung your harness up and put a fan next to it.

Hopefully it's dry," he called out.

"Thanks!" she replied as she went back inside.

Thyra made her way back into the bedroom and gathered up her clothes for the day. After she was fully dressed, she went into the garage, spotting the harness hanging up like Johnathen said it would be. She turned off the fan and squeezed the leather with her foreclaws to find it still a bit damp, but not completely drenched like it had been the night before. She took it down and started to arrange the buckles and latches in their proper places.

She reminded herself that she should really take better care of the harness. After all, it had cost her a small fortune. Leathercraft this day and age was a rare art form, and it was even more rare to find someone that would be willing to make such a complicated harness for a gryphon. Thyra roused her brown and cream feathers before settling them back down, shaking her body a bit to get the harness to fit just right.

She walked back into the kitchen to find Johnathen pouring himself another cup of coffee, finishing the pot. He grabbed the creamer out of the fridge and poured in a heavy dose. He sat down at the bar top and looked over at her. "I feel guilty staying home while you go off to work."

"Just relax and enjoy a day off for once," Thyra said to him with a smile, standing up on her hind legs to rub her smooth beak along his scruffy cheek. Johnathen wrapped one arm around the back of her neck and pulled her into a hug for a moment.

"I will try my best," he said before Thyra pulled away and disappeared down the hallway towards the front door.

The door slammed shut and Johnathen let out an exhausted sigh, putting the coffee mug down on the granite countertop. He rubbed at his temples. She was right. There was no use wallowing in self-pity or being upset. He couldn't do anything about the situation.

Johnathen took another sip of his coffee, looking out the large kitchen windows into their backyard. The bright green leaves on the trees reflected the strong golden rays of the morning sun and not a cloud was in sight.

He supposed he could work on the yard some or go into town to go get some breakfast. Anything would be better than just sitting at home, watching the television, and becoming lost in his own thoughts. He stood too quickly and winced, the sharp pain in his temples rudely reminding him of his poor decisions the night before. He went to the medicine cabinet and searched for painkillers but couldn't find any.

"Well, seems I have a reason to go out after all."

Johnathen finished off the rest of his coffee and headed for the master bathroom. The man in the mirror standing before him was not himself. He looked foreign, distant from his normal well-kept image.

He turned on the water in the sink, letting it warm up for a minute as thoughts of self-doubt crept back into his brain. He didn't deserve Thyra. She didn't need all the pain and suffering he put her through by making her live in this part of the world.

She could have gone to Europe where there were not only more of her kind, but also where the people were much more accepting of them. There she could have found a gryphon colony and settled down with another gryphon. Instead, she stayed in the south where she was constantly repressed and put down because she was different. Thyra stayed because of him, and it made him feel like he was nothing more than a burden to her.

She had so much more potential than to live out her years as a delivery girl, flying groceries around. She had said it would only be temporary, but as the years went by, it became painfully evident that nothing was going to change. Her kind was being held back here, and no matter how hard she tried, she was always going to face more obstacles than a human would.

Johnathen splashed his face with the hot water, attempting to wash the unhelpful thoughts from his mind. He let out a loud sigh and forced his thoughts in another direction.

He turned off the water and walked into the bedroom. It was a bit of a mess. There was feather dander all over the bed along with several small cream-colored feathers along the hardwood floor around the bed. He decided it would be nice to clean up for her a little bit after he got back, since she was the one that always did the cleaning. After grabbing a t-shirt and a pair of jeans, he threw on a hat to cover his messy hair and made his way to the garage.

🐾

"Fifteen orders?!" Thyra screeched in disbelief.

The covered pavilion was alive with people walking back and forth between the stands. Many of them were buying various goods from the other vendors set up in the open space. The smells of baked goods, candles and oils filled the air. People turned their attention to Thyra as she screeched a little too loudly, but the gryphoness did not seem to care.

Jimmy winced at her piercing voice and placed a pinky finger into his ears, cleaning it out. He finished packing up another large brown paper bag and set it on the counter next to the other countless bags before her. "Well, yeah, Thyra. You basically had to take most of the day off yesterday, and you know these things pile up quick."

"I know they do, but never this quickly," Thyra groaned in protest, though she was already sitting back on her hind legs and fiddling with the various latches for the satchel bags.

She grabbed a couple of large tan paper bags, stuffed with a garden of colors ranging from bright green to orange, and started to put them away inside the satchel bags hanging from her harness. Her ears flicked in agitation and she let out a loud sigh. "This is going to take 'till sundown."

"Just be happy that business is a boomin'." the old man replied as he finished ringing up the rest of the orders for delivery.

The ticket machine buzzed and clicked as it printed the receipt. Thyra sat silently, knowing that Jimmy was right. It meant more work for her than normal, but she should be happy that he was having such a thriving business and the opportunity to make more tips.

"Is Johnathen alright?" Jimmy asked casually as he proceeded to type away at the register. He didn't look at her but stared at a sheet of paper as the sound of the printer continued to clack away.

Thyra finished loading up all that she could hold and readied herself to take off on her first run. "He's fine. He just has to take a break from work is all."

The wind started to pick up, causing Thyra's brown and cream feathers to whisk in different directions. Jimmy gave a small nod and then went silent again for a short time. "If you ask me, George was always an asshole. He deserved getting socked in the face."

Thyra looked back at him in disbelief. "You know him?"

Her wide avian eyes stared over at Jimmy until he turned to face her, giving a big wrinkled grin. The short, wild white hair on top of his head wafted in the breeze. "Oh yeah. We went to high school together. I used to go to the same church as well. He was never a nice man. Really grumpy all the time. Hell, I even kicked his ass back in high school once."

Jimmy grinned wider, thinking about his younger years. "If you ask me what Johnathen did was no big deal. What kind of world do we live in that we can't act out in our violent nature against each other without everyone losin' their minds and suin' one 'nother? Back in my day, we fought like cats and dogs, and the worst we got was a talkin' to by the police."

A younger couple walked up to the stand to look over the arrangements of fruits and vegetables displayed on the crates in front of his stand. Jimmy walked out from behind his register and approached them with some kinds words.

Thyra chuckled as she made her way towards the exit of the market pavilion as she imagined what people were like in the old days compared to the way they were now. Gryphons hadn't existed back then and she was sure the world had been a completely different place without them.

Once out of the cover of the pavilion, she stretched out her broad wings and let the wind catch at her outermost primaries, letting the long finger-like feathers dance in the strong breeze. With a quick sprint forwards and a leap off of the soft ground, she was quickly in the air with a route to her first delivery location.

Chapter 13 The Invitation

Nearby birds fearful for their nests began to yell in protest, dive bombing and fluttering about around Thyra as she sat comfortably in a tall tree. She ignored the black little birds and took another bite out of the bright red apple she held in her foreclaws. It crunched in the strong bite of her beak, juices dripping down to the ground far below.

Finished, she dropped the core out of the tree and wiped her beak off with a wingtip. Sensing that their attempts to dislodge her were futile, the agitated birds finally gave up and let her be, leaving the area quiet once again.

The fog covering the hill dissipated and the sun finally showed itself after days of hiding behind cover. Thyra closed her eyes and trilled in content, letting the sun's rays warm her feathers. She enjoyed the moment for a minute, clearing her mind and taking in deep breaths of the humid morning summer air.

A series of loud beeps interrupted the tranquility of nature. Grunting, she reached into the pouch that hung around her neck and pulled out her large cellphone. It was a message from Johnathen.

Don't forget we have dinner tonight with Richard at his house.

"Richard? Richard . . ." The name was familiar, but for some odd reason her bird brain had forgotten exactly who he was.

Her phone dinged once again. *Richard is the man

who gave us the tickets. We promised that you would meet him. Just in case you forgot, bird brain.

Thyra chuckled deep in her chest, pulling out the phones sliding keyboard and began to type out a message back. *You know me too well. I should be home around noon.*

With that sent, she closed the keyboard and slipped the phone back into the leather pouch. Her stomach began to complain, grumbling loudly with hunger. One apple just wasn't enough to satisfy her, especially with how much flying she had been doing the past couple of days.

Thyra stretched out her aching wings, trembling while she balanced on the high branch. Occasionally, one of her feline hind paws threatened to slip as they weren't as good at gripping around a branch as her foretalons.

A rabbit chose that moment to dash across the open field below. Thyra's primal instincts were triggered. Her eyes grew wide and focused, following the rabbit's movements. Quickly, she jumped from her perch high in the tree.

Her broad wings closed in tight and she fell like a stone from high above. Then, just before hitting the earth, her wings snapped out wide. She flew fast and hard, angling her red tail feathers for steering and reaching with talons straight out in front of her. The rabbit squealed loudly as Thyra swooped in, landing hard on its throat.

Her blood pumped hard with hunting thrill, her wings mantled out to naturally guard her prey. The rabbit squirmed, kicking hard against Thyra's claws as it desperately tried to get away. She squeezed down against its throat until there was a loud crack and the rabbit ceased to move.

Hungrily, Thyra's head darted forward and she took a large chunk out of the rabbits back with her sharp beak, tearing the still hot and bleeding flesh from the carcass. She leaned her head back, swallowing the fresh meat whole, fur and all. Blood ran down her beak and across her cheek plumage and Thyra let out a loud sigh of relief. She closed her eyes, letting her savage side slowly fade away.

She heard a gasp and quickly turned her head to see a woman and a child standing nearby, staring at her in horror. Thyra stepped back from the rabbit. How had she not seen them?

Thyra stared back at the humans, her expression blank as she tried to think what to say. The field was relatively large, but her voice carried to them easily. "I... I am quite sorry you had to see that."

The woman clutched the little girl to her, her stare of shock quickly turning to one of anger and disgust. Thyra sat down on her haunches and reached back into the pouch to pull out a handkerchief. She used it to wipe the blood off of her beak and claws before attempting to talk once more.

"It's just . . . I-. Well you see . . . I was quite hungry and-."

"You should be ashamed of yourself! You animal!" The woman shouted, and the child began to sob.

Thyra's ears pinned back in agitation at being called an animal, but she tried to remain calm. The gryphoness looked down at the rabbit. Her eyes widened as she noticed a pink collar tied around its neck. Just then it hit her like a bag of bricks, and her eyes grew wide, beak curving into a grimace as she looked back up at the women.

"That was my daughter's birthday present!" the woman declared.

Heavily guilt creeped up in Thyra's chest and she took a step towards them. "I'm sorry! I didn't-."

"You creatures shouldn't exist!" the woman snapped. "You're an abomination!"

"Abomination?" That word was burned deep in her

brain and triggered her more than any other word in the world. She ground her beak, her blood already boiling from the hunt and now from being slurred against. "Look, I'm sorry I didn't see the collar on this thing, but-."

"You have the devil in you! Your very creation is a crime against God!" The women yelled in protest, which riled Thyra up even more. The women quickly turned around and disappeared down the trail, dragging her bawling child behind her.

Thyra watched them disappear into the woods before letting out a hawk-like angry screech. "How about next time you don't bring a pet rabbit into a field! Dumbass!"

She swiped her talons against the tall grass, tearing out clumps of soil. Before long she had calmed down, allowing other emotions to well up within her.

The gryphoness collapsed onto the soft earth and looked down at the tears falling unbidden off of her beak. Maybe they were right and she was an abomination. She never had fit in with most humans, nor was it likely she would ever be accepted as a part of normal society. It never changed, no matter how friendly she was or how well she was represented.

Thyra clenched her foreclaws, shaking as she thought of how much she wanted to leave this place. She put Johnathen through so much so that she could be his wife, and he sacrificed so much just to be with her. Was it all really worth it?

Thyra sat up, forcing her emotions under control. She used the bloodstained handkerchief to wipe the tears from around her eyes and beak before tucking it away in her pouch once again. She stood tall, taking a deep breath through her nares and walked through the grass to stand over the lifeless rabbit laying on the ground. Though her head still spun with mixed feelings, her stomach rudely reminded her of why she had done this in the first place.

She couldn't help but feel sympathetic for the little girl whose pet she had killed. Thyra had always liked the younger humans the best. Children were usually kind to her, and always wanted to pet her. They always seemed to express their emotions without any prejudices like the adults did.

Thyra sighed and dug her claws into the ground and began pulling up the soft earth. Before long, she had made a hole in the ground just big enough for the rabbit. Thyra pushed the rabbit in and looked down at the collar it was wearing. The collar had a little nametag tied to it.

"Amy." She removed the collar, repeating the name out loud while holding it in her claws.

Thyra covered the grave with some large rocks and picked up some sturdy sticks. With a little bit of rope from her pouch's neckband, she was able to tie the two sticks together to form a cross. She plunged one end of the cross into the earth at the head of the small grave and hung the collar from the top.

With that, she walked away, heading down the path towards the park's exit. Her thoughts hung heavy with every step, weighing out the events that had just unfolded. There would be repercussions to this, she was sure of it.

Just about anything out of the ordinary that she did ended up in the local news in some form. This little episode would only add more fuel to the already burning hot fire. There could be more vandalism to the house, and there would definitely be angry people, especially The Gathering members. With one last look at the little grave, she opened her wings and took to the sky, every strong wing beat elevating her higher. At least here, she was completely alone and free.

Thyra's wingtips arched out, grabbing the warm thermals that allowed her to soar freely without expending much energy. She closed her eyes, listening to the wind blowing hard against her face and feeling the sun's rays against her back.

She looked down at the city bellow with the people bustling in and out of the tall buildings. Her telescoping vision helped her to tell them apart. Many of the humans sat on park benches eating their lunches while others stood in lines at the surrounding delis. Her stomach growled loudly once again, reminding her of the ravenous state she was still in.

She angled one wing slightly downward, sending her into a lazy spiral above the city as she headed towards one of the delis that she most frequented. A nice soup would be welcome right about now, but the thought of hearty red meat made her salivate.

Thyra made her way across the town, beating her wings in quick successions of three, and then let herself glide. The buzzing city was quickly left behind and the local markets around her neighborhood began to appear in the distance. Thyra tucked in her wings and angled towards the ground, picking up speed.

At the last moment, she gave a firm backstroke and landed softly on the asphalt of a parking lot surrounded by multiple little stores. There was a grocery store, a couple of restaurants, one bar she and Johnathen frequented quite often, and a butcher shop.

People waved hello as she passed by them, being well used to her presence. Usually, she would have not thought too much about the strangers' recognition, but today a simple greeting as if she was another person was welcomed. It was a good reminder that for every human that discriminated against her, there seemed to be an equal amount that treated her with kindness and respect.

Finally, she arrived at the place she sought. The sound

of a little bell resonated in the air as Thyra pushed open the glass door to Zach's butcher shop. A short and wide man looked over the small refrigerated counter and grinned, his white apron covered in various shades of red and decorated with tidbits of meat.

He slammed his cleaver down into the wooden cutting board in front of him. There were humorous pieces of art hanging around the room, along with wooden pictures depicting the various cuts of meat for every animal.

The place was clean, its white tile always spotless, but the smell of meat hung thick in the air. Thyra enjoyed the smell, but it put Johnathen off to the point of making him sick.

"Well, if it isn't my favorite beast! Where have you been recently?" The butcher asked curiously, picking up a blood stained knife from the sink and beginning to clean it. His gray beard hung down to his chest, his eyebrows were bushy, and the light off his bald head gleamed in the light as he moved over to the register.

"I've been around, Zach, just busy with Jimmie's stand. I'm surprised you're still alive! I figured you would have had a heart attack by now," the gryphoness teased. Her heart still weighed heavy from the day's events, but she was good at hiding emotion, especially among company.

Zach had a dark sense of humor, as one would have to have working with blood and guts every day. He bellowed in laughter and reached into the cooler next to him. "I know what you're here for."

He drew out a couple of whole rabbits from the sliding glass cooler and put them down on the butcher block. Whoever his supplier was hadn't skinned them or anything. The sight of the rabbit made her stomach growl again, the taste of her earlier kill still fresh on her tongue. He picked up the meat clever and quickly relieved them of their heads.

"Sorry to disappoint ya, but this ol' ticker of mine is still going strong. I'll be sure the wife sends you an invite to the funeral when I finally do keel over, though." The sound of the cleaver hitting the wooden board made a loud thud as yet another rabbit head hit the floor, creating quite a grotesque scene.

"When you go, who the hell is going to get me fresh rabbit like you do?" Thyra retorted while standing up on her hind legs, both fore talons on the counter as she watched Zach do his work.

"I am sure you can figure it out. You could stop being lazy and go out to catch your own. It is natural for your kind to do so." Zach continued to work, picking up the knife and skinning the rabbit for her.

"I'm not sure that most people would agree with you," she replied.

The cleaver made a loud thud as he put it into the board, taking the beheaded rabbits by their feet and hanging them from a line above the sink. A small amount of dark red blood dripped down into basin as Zach turned the hot water on, letting it all rinse down the drain. He looked back to Thyra with a grin and declared, "Well, those people can suck it."

"I'll make sure and let them know that," Thyra said with a chuckle, her crest feathers standing tall and her ears perked in amusement. She enjoyed her playful banter with Zach. It was the reason she kept coming back. It put her mind at ease that there were some people in this town that at least enjoyed her company, and her business.

"Anything else for you, sweet cheeks?" he asked.

"Let's get that fillet right there for Johnathen."

She used a foreclaw to point at a nice piece of red steak under the glass. Zach nodded and wrapped it up for her to take home. Thyra threw the meat into her small satchel and reached into her pouch to pull out her wallet.

"You want the rabbits in a bag?" he asked.

"I want them in my belly, but I'll scare off customers doing that."

She gave a weak laugh to cover up the images of the little girl's face staring in horror at her and crying. *Abomination.* That word kept repeating in the back of her mind, making her hackles rise in irritation.

Thyra looked away, trying to repress the memory as Zach started clicking away at the register. They were both silent for a moment as he packed away the drained rabbits and placed them into a sack for her. He also picked up a small package of a ground pink looking meat wrapped in cellophane and threw it in as well.

"I've got somethin for you to try. Give it a taste and let me know what you think." He handed the bag over and took Thyra's credit card from her foreclaws.

She looked into the bag and cocked her head in curiosity. "What is this? Looks like ground beef, but it's too pink."

"Close! It's ground pork. You eat that raw, for breakfast, with some onions." He swiped the card and handed it back to her, leaving Thyra still clueless as to why someone would want to eat this.

"Do humans eat it like this?" Surely humans would not be able to stomach raw pork, or so she would think.

"Yeah! The krauts eat it all the time for breakfast. They put it on rolls and call it Met. I tried it myself and it's pretty damn good, once you get past the whole, it's raw, thing."

Thyra was surprised at the notion of people actually enjoying raw meat like a gryphon. She tucked the large paper bag into another satchel. "It definitely won't be a problem for me, but Johnathen on the other hand, that's a different story."

"Well tell him he's a wuss if he doesn't try it."

Thyra laughed and made her way towards the door. "I'll tell him that. See ya around."

Zach waved his goodbye and went back to business as the door closed shut behind her.

🕊

"For breakfast?!" Johnathen exclaimed from underneath his old muscle car.

The radio played softly in the background as Thyra sat next to his toolbox. The dark gray paint of the Mustang shone brightly in the light. His tools were scattered along the floor, mixed in with several boxes and old parts. With his normal work schedule, he barely had the time or the energy to get anything done with his ongoing project car. Now he had all day, every day, for the foreseeable future.

Thyra felt it was good that Johnathen kept himself busy with little projects like this to keep him from going crazy. He wheeled out from under the car and she handed a wrench over to him. "I couldn't believe it either! A human, eating raw pork? It's absurd!"

The sound of little gears on the driver echoed off the checkerboard garage floor while Johnathen wrenched away. He threw the wrench and driver down on the ground and reached up under the Ford.

"I'm not going to try it!" he grunted loudly, tugging and pulling at something which made the whole car shake on the jack stands.

Thyra laughed and got down on her chest, looking at Johnathen as he adjusted the shining new exhaust system under the vehicle. "You're going to try it! Like it or not."

Johnathen let out a loud sigh and wheeled out from under the car on his creeper before sitting up. His face and hands were covered in black from the exhaust build up. He grabbed a rag off the side of the toolbox and tried to wipe his hands clean, only smearing the dirt more.

He gave her a firm look. "No, I'm not."

Thyra, who stood a lot taller than him at that moment, peered down with icy green eyes and gave a smirk. "Yes. Yes, you are. Or else."

Johnathen raised a curious eyebrow at her. "Was that a threat?"

He was met with a response from a foreclaw that quickly pressed down on his chest. He gasped as she pinned him back down on the creeper. "Ok, ok! Fine."

Thyra chuckled and lifted her foreclaw from his chest again. Johnathen grinned back, letting out a couple of fake coughs while clutching his chest to play out the scene. "Tomorrow's breakfast then."

She nodded. "Now, that wasn't so hard, was it?"

Johnathen's phone dinged loudly and vibrated on top of the toolbox, interrupting the gryphoness. Thyra reached over and picked it up. Johnathen stood and picked up his water bottle, sipping on it while looking over at her.

"It's Richard," she told him. "He says dinner will be ready at eight."

Johnathen looked down at his watch and put the water bottle down, then made his way towards the door. "Well we better start getting ready then."

Thyra followed him up the stairs and into the living room. He continued on into the bedroom as Thyra began to put the meat away in the freezer. The shower started up and the water heater in the laundry room started to hiss slightly while she went about her business cleaning up the kitchen, organizing the dishes and placing them in their proper place.

Her claws clicked against the ceramic as she gripped the plates tightly. In her younger years, she constantly dropped plates and glasses. She'd had to resort to using just plastic or paper for the longest time. Eventually, her dexterity had improved enough that she didn't fear holding various human-made items anymore.

While Johnathen was showering, she went into the closet to pick out what they were going to wear. Johnathen was always easy to pick for. In his line of work, he'd had to collect a wardrobe of nice clothing. She picked out a dark blue button-up, a nice pair of khaki pants, and a casual black blazer from the mass of apparel.

Thyra's selections were more limited, especially in the

formal department. She owned a couple of darker dresses, a gray one complimented by a forest green garment, and a red one as well. She chose to try to match Johnathen as best she could and went with the simple gray ensemble, picking it off its hanger and tossing it on the bed next to her selection for him.

She sat back on her haunches and pulled the dress around her head first and reached her foreclaws through the sleeves. The rear was always the most difficult, working her wings through the slits on the back and then having to twist tightly around to adjust the rear of the garment as needed until everything was in place correctly. She sat back up, looking into the mirror to check the status of her feathers as the sounds of the shower stopped.

"The gray one? You don't want to show off that red dress I just got you?" Johnathen asked as he walked into the room, wearing nothing but a pair of briefs, to look at the selection of clothes that she had left on the bed.

"I didn't want to be too flashy," she said. "Even though I like how the red one compliments my tail feathers."

She turned to look in the mirror, fanning out her cinnamon-red colored tail feathers before settling them back in line. Her long, tawny-colored feline tail twitched slightly and her wings stretched out a bit, making sure the dress still fit nicely around the joints.

Johnathen threw on his clothes with ease, standing next to Thyra as he checked himself out in the mirror. "Tie or no tie?"

She reached up slightly and buttoned the two brown buttons on his blazer shut, humming while she thought for a second. "No tie."

He gave her a nod and walked into the bathroom to retrieve his hair gel, putting in a generous amount to slick his hair back. Thyra moved up behind him, standing up on her hind legs as she dragged her sharp talons carefully through his black hair. She would usually preen his hair instead but did not want the gel to get on her beak.

"You need a haircut," she observed.

"I'm thinking about letting it grow out a bit."

Thyra thought about it for a minute. Right now, if not brushed back his hair covered most of his ears and reached just above his collar. The thought of him having even longer hair was new to her.

She rubbed a talon through his scruffy beard and chuckled. "I think that would look good, but you have to trim this down at least."

He nodded in agreement and she pulled back from him, coming down on all fours once again. The electric razor buzzed loudly in the confines of the bathroom. Once done, Johnathen rubbed his fingers along the now groomed beard and brushed the little hairs off the front of his shirt as he turned to walk out.

"Looks much better," she commented.

With their preparations complete, Johnathen and Thyra gathered up their things and walked into the garage. Johnathen went over to a box hanging on the wall to collect the Ford's key.

Thyra's ear tufts perked up in excitement as he opened the garage door. "You're really going to take it out?"

"Yeah, ol' girl hasn't ran in a while," he replied. "Plus, I want to hear the new exhaust."

Thyra pranced happily over to the side passenger door and threw it open. The interior was just as immaculate as the outside. The old dark carpet and black vinyl seats looked the same as they had when they left the factory. She carefully got in, making sure her claws did not dig into the seats.

Johnathen slid into the driver's side, shutting the door

behind him and wrapped his hands around the hefty wooden steering wheel He gave a soft sigh, put the key into the starter, and gave it a turn.

The starter motor cranked loudly, whirring multiple times as the engine sputtered and stopped. Johnathen grimaced, pumped the gas pedal a few times, and tried once more. The car jerked to one side as the thrumming symphony of a roaring V8 filled the garage, bringing a smile to the couple.

Johnathen looked over at Thyra, beaming from ear to ear before giving it a couple more revs. She chuckled as her ears rang while the eight cylinder engine sang its baritone melody. Johnathen eased out the clutch, making the large metal beast roll slowly out of the garage and into the no longer-quiet streets of the night.

Chapter 14 The Offer

The Mustang's headlights shone against metal as Johnathen came to a slow stop in front of a large gate. The loping idle of the sizable engine created quite a racket in the high-class neighborhood. Suddenly, the gate began to open, giving access to the mansion's driveway.

The vast house was well lit at night. Multiple outdoor floodlights shone against the house's exterior, showing off its magnificent beauty. Johnathen drove up the drive and then cut the engine off, leaving the area silent once again. The sounds of crickets chirping all around filled the cool night air while the couple exited the vehicle.

"Think of the power bill this guy has to pay," Johnathen commented while standing next to the Mustang, bewildered by the stature of the mansion.

Five huge stone columns decorated the front entrance, holding the roof of the deck up. Thyra was impressed by the exterior of the home but was more interested in what was inside. They approached the porch, but before they were close enough to knock, the front door opened before them. A youthful, well-built man stepped outside and smiled.

"Could hear you coming from a mile away!" he exclaimed, his short blond hair shining in the bright front porch lights.

The man walked over to Thyra, his eyes looked to hers with interest. Thyra froze and sat down on her haunches as the young man bent down, taking her foreclaw into his hand.

"Greetings, Thyra. I've been looking forward to meeting you," the man said with an aristocratic British accent, shaking her talons with excitement. Thyra chuckled politely and smiled, giving him a nod. "You look simply dashing tonight, may I add."

The gryphoness' cere took on a slight red tint as he complimented her, a gryphon's way of blushing. He looked up at Johnathen and stood straight to shake his hand as well. "And you must be Johnathen. Thank you so much for coming! I am Richard. It is a pleasure to make your acquaintance!"

The man's accent was pleasant and entertaining, which made them chuckle in amusement.

"We are very happy to be here, Richard. Thank you for inviting us," Johnathen replied.

"Of course!" Richard's eyes glanced over to the gray Mustang sitting in the driveway and whistled. "Is that a sixty-nine Mach-1?" He asked Johnathen.

"It is, all original too." Johnathen replied with a proud smile. Richard looked over it for a minute and turned his attention to Johnathen. "Are you looking to sell it?"

Johnathen laughed and shook his head, "No thank you. It was my dad's. Kind of a sentimental thing."

Richard shrugged his shoulders, "Oh well! Please, come in!" he said and turned around, heading back into his home. The couple followed and stepped into the mansion's lobby. Thyra's beak dropped open and Johnathen's eyes grew as they looked around the spacious interior.

At the center of the lobby was an immense stone fountain that created quite a nice ambiance in the room. A grand chandelier hung from the ceiling, casting enough light to brighten the room and there were two large staircases leading up to the next floor on either side.

"It's just this way," Richard said, a slight smile on his face at the couple's gawking. He led them down a long corridor, the sounds of claws and shoes echoing off the walls. Suits of shining armor stood against the walls, all from various centuries. Johnathen had so many questions but figured they would be best asked at a later time.

They continued down the corridor and after what felt like minutes of walking, arrived at the main living room. At the center were a couple of large couches. A man stood by one of them, his back straight and gaze formal. His black and white suit was well kept and ironed out perfectly. He held a silver tray with small crystal glasses on top.

Richard took two glasses from the tray and offered them to Thyra and Johnathen. Richard noted the confusion in the gryphoness' gaze and sat back in a leather recliner by a burning fireplace.

"What were those metal people?" Thyra asked out loud, puzzled by the metal structures in human form they had passed on the way in.

"Those are suits of armor for knights, my dear. Fifteenth to sixteenth century to be exact," Richard told the curious gryphoness. Johnathen turned to face Thyra with shock on his face, really confused as to why she did not recognize what they were.

"You didn't know? We just watched *A Knight's Tale* last week!" Johnathen exclaimed.

Thyra's eartufts perked as she made the connection. "Oh! That's right. They just look so different in real life. I guess I need to study more human history." Thyra had studied a lot of history in her free time, but it mainly was about America. Not having a formal education, she was not aware of the histories of other countries.

Richard smiled. "Warriors of great strength and skill would wear these suits. Back in the olden days, they did not possess artillery like the modern weapons we have today. They fought with only primitive weaponry: swords, spears, arrows, and the like." He gestured to the couch behind her, "Please, do sit."

Thyra hopped up onto the sofa across from Richard and made herself comfortable as Johnathen did the same. "They would wear those things? Wouldn't it be tough to move around?"

Richard nodded and took a sip of the dark brown liquor in his crystal glass. "That is true, Thyra! They were a bit unwieldy. But it was worth it. Against peasants with crude weapons they were almost invincible on the battlefield."

The well-dressed servant grabbed a small wooden box out of a glass humidor and brought it over to Johnathen. Johnathen reached into the box that was offered and pulled out a fat cigar with a smile on his face.

"Cubans?!" Johnathen said with excitement.

Richard gave him a hearty chuckle as the butler carefully cut off one end of the cigar, then struck a match and held it out to Johnathen. "Most certainty, my good boy! Only the finest."

Johnathen put the immense cigar to his lips and puffed as the butler lit the end, creating a cloud of smoke. Thyra took a sip of her liquor, trying to decide whether or not to glare as he partook of the cigar. He looked back and gave her a small shrug. "It would have been rude to decline, hon."

Thyra huffed and turned back to face Richard as the large room filled with the smell of fine burning tobacco. Everyone was quiet for a short time, and the only sounds were the crackling of the fire.

Finally, Richard broke the silence. "Now John, may I

call you John?"

"Only if I can call you Rick," Johnathen replied.

Richard laughed at this. "We have a deal."

The butler moved to stand next to Rick, quiet as a ghost. Once Rick had finished his drink and placed it on the silver platter the butler was holding, the man quickly turned and walked out the door.

Rick leaned back in his chair. "So, John, how did the two of you meet? There has to be an interesting story."

Johnathen looked over at Thyra. She perked her ear tufts and then folded them back, a little embarrassed by their origin story. She giggled, looking at Johnathen with affection. "We don't tell it too often because it's a bit embarrassing."

Rick gauged their reactions and leaned forward. "Alright, I was just making small talk but now you two have me intrigued!"

Johnathen rubbed the back of his head nervously and chuckled. "Well, I don't mind telling it. I like our story."

"Go on then," Rick encouraged and took another drag of his cigar. The butler entered the room again with more drinks and carefully began handing them out.

"Thank you," Johnathen told the man, taking the glass before beginning his story. "It all started about ten years ago. We were young, and I was a freshman in college."

Johnathen began his story, looking at Thyra with a smile. She looked just as beautiful back then as she did now. He sat back on the couch, kicking his feet on to the ottoman while having another puff of his own cigar. Thyra sipped from her new crystal glass and chuckled as Johnathen started to tell the tale. She could remember it vividly.

"Law school isn't cheap, and I was working in a coffee shop at the time, trying to make ends meet. One day she walked in. I couldn't tear my eyes away from her if I tried. I was mesmerized, but I didn't have the guts to talk to her."

He laughed and took another sip of the strong whiskey. His head swirled both from the second stiff drink and the memories coming back to him.

"I'd always been fascinated with gryphons ever since I was a kid. They were a new species when I was growing up and were everywhere in the news. Some of what was said was good and some bad, but I always liked them. I watched them on TV, saw them at gryphball games, and read about them in magazines. But I had never seen one in person before that day.

"I was mad at myself for not approaching her the first time. But she kept coming back. Thyra would come in at the same time every day, always order the same thing, and sit down in the same spot by the window. Her beak was always buried in a book. Accounts of the Civil War. I can still remember the cover."

Johnathen put down the drink and felt Thyra's claws intertwine with his fingers, squeezing them gently. He looked over at her and smiled while Rick sat up, mesmerized by his story.

"I kept telling myself this is going to be the day. I'm going to do it. Then one day, I finally worked up the guts to talk to her. She came in, got her usual coffee, and sat down in her corner window seat. I had a tray of some sweets I got from the kitchen along with some milk. I made a beeline straight for her, my heart throbbing in my throat, and then I tripped over someone's foot."

"Cakes and creamer went everywhere!" Thyra said.

Johnathen mimed the tray flying up into the air and they all laughed at the thought of him completely making a fool of himself in front of all those people and Thyra. He shook his head.

"I ruined a lady's shirt and some poor old man got a bath of milk. I looked up off the floor to see Thyra leaning down, trying to help me up. She was laughing at me and smiling. I've never been so embarrassed in my life."

"I found it hilarious, but he didn't." Thyra added in. "Johnathen just gathered his things and ran to the back. I didn't see him for a couple days after that, which was unusual, because every day I came in, he was always there staring at me. I admit I thought he was a creep at first, but he looked like he wanted to talk with me. I figured he was just curious about gryphons, so the next time I saw him he was outside the coffee shop smoking and I approached him."

"I was so nervous when I saw her walk up." Johnathen replayed the memory in his head. "But I had already told myself if I saw her again, I would ask her out."

"I admit, it was a bit shocking. I'd never considered dating a human, but Johnathen seemed really nice. A lot nicer than most. We gryphons were not the most popular things back then. So, I agreed."

"We went on our first date by the river," Johnathen said. "I was completely broke, but I spent every dollar I had on that first date trying to impress her. Apparently, I must have done something right."

"He was no gryphon, but I found myself enjoying his company. At first, it was a little unnatural feeling, but that changed the more we went out."

Rick was beaming ear to ear as he finished up the last of his drink. The butler came back into the room, interrupting the silence.

"Excuse me. The dinner is ready."

"Very good, Jeffrey! Thank you, my good sir," Rick said. He placed his crystal glass down on the table next to him and stood. Johnathen took that as an invitation to stand,

and did so, holding onto Thyra's foreclaw as she hopped off the couch and placed the empty glass down on the coffee table.

Rick turned to head out of the room, motioning for them to follow. "I certainly hope the two of you are hungry! I had the chefs prepare some exquisite delights for tonight."

The couple walked behind Rick and made their way into the dining room. Their eyes grew large at the sight of the selection of meats, vegetables, and bread upon the grand dining table. The butler stood in the corner of the room, holding a wine bottle. Rick walked over to his seat at the end of the table and motioned over to a unique, comfortable-looking pillow standing slightly off the ground with wooden legs.

"I thought this should be more to your liking, Thyra. I have a man in Atlanta that custom makes these for my gryphon guests. That one was built just for you."

Rick smiled and sat down across from them quietly. Thyra sat down on the cushion on her haunches as Johnathen sat down next to her at the table.

"Really? Thank you! It's better than trying to sit in a chair, and much more comfortable than the couch cushion Johnathen bought for me." She glanced over at Johnathen while the waiter walked over to pour her and Johnathen a glass of wine.

"I don't know any custom furniture makers!" Johnathen exclaimed as he sipped his wine glass.

"Jeffrey will make sure to have it delivered to your home tomorrow." Rick said. Rick motioned over to the selection of meats on the table. "Please, help yourselves while it's hot."

There was pork and beef, sliced out and arranged nicely on large serving plates. One particular meat caught

Thyra's attention the most, several cooked quail breasts. She picked up the tray and pulled it towards her with glee. Richard and Johnathen took a couple slices of the beef and vegetables while Thyra picked up a fork and a knife to begin cutting into the quail meat.

"You don't have to do that. Go ahead and use your claws. I imagine its cumbersome for you to use utensils." Rick said to which Thyra gave a big beak grin. She tore the meat apart with her claws and beak, trying to be as civil as possible.

She let out gentle thrills of satisfaction while swallowing down a beak full of the moist and tender quail. "This is delicious! I need to get the recipe from your chef."

Rick and Johnathen began to cut their selections of meat and ate with Thyra, smiling at Thyra's apparent enjoyment.

"I will certainly ask the chef for you," Rick replied as Thyra ate. "Although I can't promise anything. He is a bit tight-lipped when it comes to his recipes."

"All of this is amazing. Thank you again for inviting us," Johnathen commented while taking a sip of his red wine.

"It is a pleasure to be in your company," Rick said with a polite nod. "I did, however, invite you both here for a reason."

Thyra and Johnathen stopped eating for a second and gave Rick their full attention. He sat calmly and put down his eating utensils to look over at Thyra with a big smile.

"I have seen you fly many times on your deliveries. Your build is fantastic, and you move very well on wing. You even have a flair for the dramatic the way you land. Every time I see you I have wondered to myself, why are you only delivering groceries? Why are you not pursuing other options? You have so much potential for greater avenues."

Thyra flattened her ear tufts against her skull in embarrassment. The question put a heavy load on her, making her feathers fall flat. She had thought about this often. She knew that she could be much more than just a delivery girl, but she was happy with her job and wasn't in it for the money necessarily. Although, with the way things were going at the moment, more money would be nice.

"I tried some other things, but it seems that humans aren't too fond of a gryphon having a high-paying job. I wanted to go to college, but none would accept me. They said they didn't have the seats and every class was always booked. An obvious lie," she said with a loud sigh.

Johnathen grew irritated at Rick's question. The man had been kind thus far but putting Thyra down was something he did not take lightly. Why go to all the trouble of inviting them all this way just to belittle her? He shot Rick a glare and turned to place a comforting hand on Thyra's neck. He put a finger under her beak, pulling it up a little to look into her striking green eyes. "You always try your best, Thyra. It doesn't matter what other people think. You-."

"Please allow me to interrupt again," said Richard hurriedly. "I had no intention to belittle you, Thyra. I only asked the question because I wish to offer you a proposal."

Thyra and Johnathen both looked back over to Rick, surprised by the statement.

"As you no doubt have seen, I am quite a wealthy man. Was born with a silver spoon in my mouth, as you all say around here. The reason for this is because of my parents' entrepreneur spirit. They built a financial empire and I have carried on their legacy. My family owns many businesses across the globe. Although, there is always one thing that interested me most, gryphball."

Johnathen and Thyra gave him perplexed looks while the butler made his rounds, filling the wine glasses with little interest in the conversation at hand. Thyra opened her beak to say something during the pause, but Rick cut back in.

"You see, I own a couple Gryphon League teams, and we happen to be short a player on one of them, the Georgia Red-Tails to be exact. What I was hoping is that you would come and play for them."

Thyra's eyes grew wide as she realized what he was asking of her. Her feathers roused in excitement and she stood up straight, tail flicking all about behind her. "You're saying, you want me to be on the team? A professional gryphball team?!"

Richard gave her a sly grin and took another sip from his wine glass. "Precisely, my dear. What do you say?"

She looked over at Johnathen, beak curved into a big smile as Johnathen looked back, dumbfounded by the wild proposition. He gave her an excited nod and Thyra turned back around quickly to face Richard, her crest feathers raised straight up frantic energy.

"Yes! A million times yes!"

"Splendid!" Richard said with a grin and raised his glass for a toast.

Thyra was so thrilled; she could barely hold the glass with her foreclaws.

"To a good season and partnership." Rick gave the toast as the sound of glasses clinked together in celebration.

Chapter 15 Court Date

Keith slapped Johnathen on the shoulder as they stood in front of the courthouse. The sun was hidden behind a thick layer of clouds this morning, casting a dreary shadow upon the city. People buzzed all around them, walking into the city hall and down the street to their various destinations. Johnathen took a deep breath and picked up his leather briefcase.

"It's just a misdemeanor case," Keith reminded him in a reassuring tone as they walked across the street. He opened one of the sizable wooden doors. "We were doing those in our internship. Easy stuff."

Johnathen snorted. "And I have that same butterflies in my stomach feeling now as I did with those old cases."

The polished concrete floors shone brightly, and a large crest of the town's logo was centered in the middle. Well-dressed citizens sat on leather covered benches, talking among themselves. It was the smaller of Macon's courthouses, which handled most of the misdemeanor cases. Johnathen and Keith both felt a fair amount of déjà vu as they walked through the building. Most of their internship and many years after were spent here, defending small claims cases just like today's.

"Morning fellas," said the guard that was standing by the metal detector. He was a sizeable man and Johnathen knew him well.

Keith and Johnathen put down their briefcases on the

wooden table next to him and walked through the metal detector.

"Morning, Kyle. How's the kids?" Johnathen asked the guard, doing his best to act like it was any normal day.

Kyle smiled and opened both of the briefcases, quickly checking them before handing them back. "Growing like weeds. Never knew I'd have to spend so much on clothes."

"I hear you," Johnathen said. In truth, he had very little experience with children, but that was the last thing on his mind at the moment. He waved to the guard and kept on walking with Keith, anxiety rising within him the closer they drew to the courtroom.

They continued up a central staircase in the middle of the lobby until they reached the main courtrooms. With a deep sigh, Johnathen pushed open the timber doors and continued inside.

A sizable gathering of people sat in the rows of benches, looking to spectate the case. Johnathen recognized a couple of familiar faces, but none of them were people he considered friends. This was feeling more real now. His heart began to race in his throat, making his ears ring. Every step took an eternity.

As he moved towards his seat on the defendant's bench, Johnathen glanced over to the right and almost froze in place. The bishop of his old church sat not far away, staring at Johnathen with a malicious smile. Mathew's dark brown eyes locked to Johnathen's pupils, glaring right into his very soul.

Instantly, Johnathen forgot his fear. His blood began to boil. Pure, searing rage filled him and consumed his thoughts. At that moment he wanted nothing more than to leap at the Bishop and strangle him in front of all these people, to watch Matthew turn purple as he slowly suffocated.

Keith noticed the expression on his face and turned to notice Matthew sitting among the pews. A shiver went down Keith's spine at the sight of the aging white-haired man, and he gripped Johnathen's shoulder. "Forget about him."

Clenching his fists, Johnathen turned away. They both entered the small gate separating the audience from the defendant and sat down at the table before the judge's bench. Johnathen was gritting his teeth, unable to unclench his jaw.

It had been years since he had seen Mathew face-to-face and he had let himself forget how much he disliked the man. He took a deep breath, trying to clear his mind and put on a professional demeanor. Johnathen had feared that Mathew would be in the courtroom today, but that still did not prepare him for the revulsion he felt now.

Keith placed his briefcase on the desk, opening the latches and taking a couple of papers from the inside. He whispered to Johnathen, "Relax. You know he only showed up to make you choke, but you're better than that. I know you are."

Johnathen slowly opened up his briefcase and began to pull an envelope out, taking deep breaths. As he began to review the notes, he said under his breath, "The man would like nothing more than to see me in handcuffs."

"Today is not that day," Keith said with a confident grin and slapped Johnathen on the back.

The main entrance door opened once more and everyone turned their heads to look at the newcomer. Johnathen spared him only a brief glance before turning back around to face the Judge's bench.

The old man was wearing a bandage over his nose. He was walking gingerly, playing up the age angle for the watchers. George sat down with his lawyer at the desk next to them and glared at Johnathen.

Keith huffed and bent his head down to whisper to Johnathen once again. "He's playing the victim card. It's been weeks and he's still wearing a bandage on his nose."

Johnathen gave him a nod and put down his notes. "As I expected. It's an easy win for him if the judge is convinced."

Keith lifted his head again to watch George and the lawyer talking, and his eyes grew a little in surprise. He leaned down to Johnathen once again. "You see they got one of the Thomson Law boys? They're the most expensive lawyers in the city."

Johnathen lifted his head again to look over. It was definitely one of their rival firm's lawyers. Expensive. George might have had a lot of money, but Johnathen greatly suspected Matthew was behind that too.

"It doesn't matter who they have. It's a petty case. This will be over before lunch time," Johnathen said before summoning up all his confidence and taking a stand.

Keith chuckled approvingly, "Now that's the Johnny I know."

One of the blended-in wooden doors opened beside the judge's stand. A broad and dark man wearing a well-starched uniform walked out. He stood in front of the bench and looked around at the small crowd of people.

"Please stand for the Honorable Judge Chelsey Winter"

Everybody in the room came to their feet while a dark woman walked out from behind the door. Judge Winter was in her late fifties and had short curly black hair. She wore a stern look on her face. She climbed the judge's stand, towering over everybody, and sat down.

"Please be seated," she said with a calm and

professional demeanor. Everyone took their seats as instructed and sat silently while the judge put on her glasses and began to read over the literature on her desk.

"Mister Arkwright. You are being tried for a simple assault case. How do you plead?"

Johnathen stood and looked straight at the judge. "Not guilty."

The Judge nodded, her curly black hair moving slightly as she turned to face George and his lawyer. "The plaintiff may now give their opening statement."

&

Thyra sat on the ledge of a tall building overlooking the courthouse. The cool wind picked up, ruffling through her feathers in the dim light of the overcast day. Summer had slowly faded, and fall was creeping up quickly. She shivered from the cold chill that ran up her back.

She took another bite of the sandwich she had just purchased from the deli across the street and swallowed it down. She could only imagine how Johnathen was feeling right then. He had been acting cool and collected earlier, but how nervous he must be?

Johnathen was a good lawyer, but it was a bit different when his own life was on the line. The fines and sentence of such a small assault case might not be that severe but going to jail for just one day could result in him losing his job. Law was the only thing Johnathen knew, and he would be lost without it.

Thyra finished the small sandwich and gripped her claws on the stone edge of the building, letting out a loud sigh. She hated that she was powerless to help. Her phone dinged loudly in her pouch, distracting her from her negative thoughts. She pulled the phone from her pouch and tilted her head in confusion at the odd phone number the text had come from.

Hey! This is Isabell, the gryphon that you met at the gryphball game the other day. Was seeing if you wanted to hang out tonight!

The memory of the brightly-colored gryphoness came back to her right away. Thyra smiled, the distraction of Isabell helping to lift her ill mood. She thought Johnathen would probably enjoy getting away for the night as well.

Thyra turned the phone sideways and flipped open the keyboard. It took Thyra a little while to slowly type out the words. Her talons pecked away at the letters until the message was eventually sent. *Hey Isabell! Johnathen and I would love to go out tonight. Where and when?*

A few seconds later the response came back. *How about this place called Stevarino's at eight? It's not too far from you, halfway between Macon and Warner Robbins. They have really good bar food and plenty to drink!*

Thyra blinked in shock at how quickly the other gryphoness typed out the reply. In all Thyra's years of practicing with keyboards, she could never get any faster.

Eight sounds good!

Thyra slid her phone closed and put it back into the pouch. It would be a pleasant evening getting away from everything. She looked down at the ground from atop of the Grand Opera House. People bustled around the city's streets on their lunch break, piling into cafes and sandwich shops.

Her ear tufts perked up as the town clock struck noon, the loud bells filling the city streets with a pleasant melody. It was time for a court recess.

She watched as a small group of people began to exit the city hall until spying Johnathen and Keith walking out.

Thyra launched off the rooftop as quickly as she could and glided down towards them. People turned their heads to see the gryphoness landing softly in the grass of the courtyard.

"Thyra! Good to see ya!" Keith said and rubbed under her beak. Thyra chuckled a bit and nodded to him, standing almost chest height with Keith.

"Good to see the both of you," Thyra said cheerfully, trying to boost the mood and stay positive. Her eyes locked on to Johnathen's, judging his disposition. He seemed to be disgruntled, but confident. He looked back at Thyra and smiled to reassure the worrying gryphoness.

"So?" Thyra finally asked, sitting down in front of them as they took a seat on a park bench.

"It's going well," Keith assured her. "Just a bit stressful. They tried pulling some bullshit, but we came well prepared."

Johnathen looked around before continuing. "Matthew is here. They were pulling out all the tricks in the book."

Just the mention of Mathew's name made Thyra's crest feathers rouse in irritation. She clicked her beak with displeasure and looked around as if expecting him to stroll right up to them. "He better not show his face around me. I'd pluck the eyeballs out of that ugly skull of his."

Her chest plumage was puffed up, tail thrashing around mindlessly while she thought about the bishop. Johnathen grabbed both of her cheeks and rubbed them gently, bringing her attention to him once more. He leaned in and kissed her beak with a grin. "I know you would, my little killing machine."

Thyra trilled in content and rubbed her cheek against his before Keith cleared his throat. They both sat back again, realizing that some of these people had come from the courtroom.

"Oh! Before I forget." She reached into her large satchel and brought out two sandwiches. "BLT for Johnathen, and pastrami for Keith."

Keith and Johnathen both grinned and thanked Thyra for the food, taking the subs from her claws. The guys quickly began to eat their lunch, stuffing their faces with ravenous hunger.

"Oh, Johnathen," Thyra said. "You remember Isabell, the gryphoness we met at the game?"

Johnathen took another bite of his sub before nodding in response, mouth too full to say anything.

"She just texted me and asked if we wanted to go out and have a drink with her tonight. I told her we would."

Johnathen just nodded again as he ate, which made Thyra raise an eye ridge. "You alright with that?"

Johnathen finished off the last bite and swallowed.

"Let's see how this goes. If it goes like I think, I could use a night away, and a couple drinks after all this."

Just then everybody began to stand and head towards the doors. Johnathen and Keith stood as well, watching as the small crowd poured into the court building. Keith waved goodbye and followed inside, leaving Thyra and Johnathen by themselves.

"Be careful in there. Keep a level head," Thyra said with a concerned tone. She knew he was on edge, especially with Matthew being among the spectators.

He put his hand on Thyra's head, ruffling up her crest feathers with a little smile. "Don't you worry. We have this in the bag."

With Thyra reassured, Johnathen turned and followed Keith back into the building. She sat for a minute, staring at the entrance, wishing that she could go inside the courtroom with them. Unfortunately, there were laws against gryphons in the court room. They were not allowed to be present at court cases.

Thyra glanced around the street, noticing that most of the people from the lunch rush had already gone. The streets were quiet except for a few cars passing by. Johnathen would tell her when the case was over, but until then she had some time to kill and she only had one errand to do for the rest of the day.

She decided it was time to go talk to Jimmy about putting in her notice. It had been a week since she got the offer to join the Gryphon League and she would start training very soon. She had shown up to work as usual for the past week and had been putting off telling Jimmy about it. Thyra let out a sigh, thinking of how upset Jimmy was going to be about her quitting, especially when his business was doing so well. It was the right thing to do, though. She could not be training for the Gryphon League and working full time for him too.

With the market in mind, Thyra leaped from the ground and gave a couple of hard backstrokes of her broad wings. She quickly gained altitude and soared over the buildings, heading out towards the outskirts of town. She hit some turbulence, the wind gusting wildly in different directions, tugging at her outermost primaries and forcing her to work for a steady glide. She shivered, the colder air higher up blowing straight into her down feathers. She was already starting to miss the fire-blazing heat of the summer.

Thyra spotted the gleaming silver metal roof of the large market pavilion in the distance and alighted herself for descent. She came in low and slow, tilting her wings back for a soft landing onto the green grass. There weren't many cars in the parking lot. The market was quite empty compared to the mid-summer weeks.

She made her way over to the stand. Jimmy spotted her approach from a distance. The old man perked up from the sight of her and Thyra gave him a smile.

"Well I'll be. What are you doin' here? Ain't this your day off with that big court case?"

Thyra chuckled and walked into the stand next to him, noticing most of his baskets and shelves were empty of produce. "Looks like you had a good day today."

The old man scratched his leathery cheek and gave a hearty laugh. "Yeah, you could say that. Not much produce to begin with, but I sold most of it. Had to have a couple young boys run the groceries though. It ain't even half the orders you had, and they still couldn't keep up!"

Thyra laughed and gave her wings a little flutter. "Well these do help me a lot. It's something they don't have."

Jimmy smiled to her and looked down at his paper, scribbling some things down, his crazy white hair blowing easily with the wind. "It wouldn't matter if those boys were driving drag cars. They still couldn't outrun you."

Thyra grinned at his compliment, then looked down at her talons with a frown. She drew circles in the dirt nervously as her ear tufts fell flat to her skull.

The silence made Jimmy look back over to her with worry. He knew that usually she would reply with a witty comeback or something smart to say, but she sat, silent as a church mouse. "What's wrong Thyra?"

She took a deep breath and looked back up at the old man. His facial expression was caring, and it made guilt rise within her. "I . . . I have to quit working for you."

Jimmy seemed unfazed by what she said. He simply looked back down and clicked away at the calculator. "I knew this day was coming. You can't be working for an old geezer like me for forever."

Thyra walked around the counter and sat down close to him. He always began to grow distant when he was upset. She had been working for him for the greater part of a decade and learned to read him like a book. "You know I love working for you, but I had a job offer I couldn't refuse."

He put down his pencil and looked over at Thyra, who was now wearing an excited smile on her beak. "Jimmy, I was asked to be a part of the Gryphon League."

Jimmy perked up at this, his blank expression lightening. He placed a hand on top of her head, scratching the top of her crest feathers and ruffling them up. "Well, I'll be darned! That's always what you wanted, wasn't it? I'm happy for ya, gal."

Thyra gave a nod and a gentle thrill to him in response. "Ever since I was a gryphlet."

Jimmy stood up out of his chair and walked towards the back of the stand. He pulled out his cash box and unlocked it.

"I hate to lose my best employee, but I got something for ya."

Jimmy turned around and held out his hand. Dangling from his fingertips was a small golden necklace. A four leaf clover hung at the end of it.

"This was my brother's lucky necklace. He always wore it when he played baseball and said it helped him win games. He wore the thing 'till the day he died."

"Are you sure?" Thyra said in shock. "You want to give this family heirloom to me?"

Jimmy shrugged. "I ain't got a use for luck. Don't believe in it, personally. But who knows? It might help ya out."

Thyra gratefully took the small necklace and held it in her gray foreclaws, then stood up on her hind feet and wrapped her talons around the back of his neck, pulling the old man into a big hug. He smiled and gave her a big hug back, squeezing the gryphoness tight.

"Thank you. For everything," she said before letting herself back down onto all fours.

Jimmy smiled and took his seat once again. "Don't be actin' like this is goodbye or nothin'. You better come back and buy produce from time to time, ya hear?"

Thyra chuckled and turned around to leave, tail flicking about behind her. "Sure thing. I'll be seeing you, you old geezer."

Jimmy smiled and watched her take wing out through the front entrance, disappearing into the cloudy sky.

Chapter 16 Clucking Hens

Johnathen cut off the ignition to the rumbling engine and sat quietly for a minute, observing the weather-beaten green building in front of him. There were motorcycles parked all along the front of the building, and neon signs for various beer brands flickered dimly in the night. A couple of rough-looking men stood outside, laughing and smoking, talking about their night's escapades.

"Are you sure this is the place?" he asked Thyra with a bit of uncertainty in his voice.

She looked down at her phone and gave a nod. "Looks like it."

Johnathen opened the heavy metal car door and got out, Thyra doing the same. The men stopped having their conversation and looked over at the two, puzzled by their appearance.

"I think we're a bit overdressed," Johnathen whispered to Thyra as they opened the doors to the dimly lit bar inside. Thyra had decided to wear her green dress and Johnathen wore one of his suit jackets.

A cloud of smoke hit them in the face, making Thyra's eartufts pin back in disgust. There were billiard tables scattered around the large open room, with a large bar to one side and televisions hanging on every wall. A couple of people turned their heads to look at the two standing in the doorway and sticking out like sore thumbs. Rock music and sounds of people echoed in the room as they cheered on their favorite Gryphon League team on the television.

"Hey Thyra!" came a shout out from across the room.

They turned their heads to catch the sight of the gryphoness they were here to meet. Thyra almost didn't recognize her. In the sun Isabell's feathers had shifted in brilliant color, but in the dim light of the bar her feathers seemed almost black. She waved them over with a foreclaw and they began to make their way to her. Johnathen accidentally bumped into a large burly man playing billiards and quickly apologized but not without receiving a few angry glares.

Isabell let out a loud laugh from her long and slender beak. "What in the hell are you two wearing?"

Johnathen and Thyra sat down at the small booth in the corner of the room and took another look around, feeling extremely uneasy and out of place.

"Apparently not the right thing," Johnathen replied. He made eye contact with one of the pool players by accident and hurriedly looked away, returning his attention to the colorful gryphoness.

Isabell wore a ragged looking purple Metallica T-shirt with large holes cut out for her wings. Up close, her plumage shifted from purple to a twilight black in the dim overhead lighting. She had piercings in her nares and little studs clipped to some of her head feathers.

She wrapped her dark talons around the glass mug handle and poured the golden contents of her beer into her beak before laying it back down. She practically had to shout so they could hear her. "Definitely not!" Just then the waitress came over to the table. She wasn't in uniform, wearing just a plain shirt and jeans with her long blond hair hanging unbound around her shoulders.

She smirked and nodded at Isabell. "Who are these

strangers, darlin'? They look like lost puppies."

Isabell laughed once again and motioned to Thyra. "This is Thyra! I met her at a gryphball match a couple weeks back, and this is John, her husband."

"Husband?" The waitress raised an eyebrow, her curiosity piqued. "No shit? I ain't never seen one of y'all hitched with a human before."

Thyra and Johnathen exchanged a nervous glance, not sure where this was heading.

"First time I have seen it too!" said Isabel. "But they make a cute couple."

All Johnathen and Thyra could do was smile uneasily and take the odd compliment.

The waitress looked over them, giving them a friendly smile back before reaching into her back pocket and pulling out a small notebook. She looked over to Thyra. "So, what'll it be, hun?"

The gryphoness roused her almond brown feathers with a skittish cough. "I... I will take a scotch. Neat."

Both Isabell and the waitress raised their eyebrows at Thyra's choice of such a strong drink. "Alright, little flower. One scotch for the lady and what about you, mister nine- to-five?"

"Make it two," Johnathen said, raising two fingers. The waitress chuckled at his short response, then nodded and walked off towards the bar. Johnathen glanced at Isabell, "You come here often?"

"All the time. This is my favorite little dive. Everyone's real friendly here."

They did not seem all that friendly to Johnathen. In fact, these were the types of troublemakers that he saw on trial in the courthouse.

Isabell took another swig of her beer and looked over

at Thyra, whose feathers had collapsed out of nervousness. "I hear you're going to be in the Gryphon League this coming season!"

Thyra blinked at the gryphoness, as if just snapping back from reality.

"Oh yes! I forgot to tell you. I have been trying to get back into shape for the past couple weeks, but it's been all at home. I have a personal trainer now telling me what to eat and how much to exercise every day. He wouldn't be too happy with me having alcohol, but he doesn't have to find out. I'm really excited to begin the real training next week at the stadium."

"You mean you haven't even been to the stadium yet?" Isabell asked in a bit of confusion. The waitress walked by and sat their drinks down on the table before making a hasty retreat back to the bar.

Thyra shook her head and wrapped her dark talons around the glass. "No. Not yet. Seems I need to be conditioned first. I guess I was extremely out of shape." She brought the drink to her beak and took a gulp of the whiskey. Her expression quickly soured. Johnathen and Isabell grinned as Thyra coughed and looked at the glass in disgust. "W...what is this vile drink?!"

Johnathen took a drink from his own glass and laughed. "That, dear, is bottom-shelf scotch."

Isabell snorted and sipped her beer through her long beak. "Not as good as that fancy stuff you're used to, huh?"

Thyra grimaced and slid over her glass to Johnathen. "Here you take this filth away from me."

Isabell nudged Johnathen with a wing to get his attention. "You ever expect to marry such a high maintenance hen such as herself?"

"If I'm high maintenance, it's his own damned fault!"

Thyra quickly retorted with a flush of her nares.

He shrugged. "Can't disagree with that. I spoil her too much."

The waitress walked back over, having seen Thyra's reaction to the liquor, and asked in an almost mocking tone. "Seems that was too much for ya, flower. May I suggest a Miller Light?"

Thyra gave an embarrassed nod and the waitress was off once again. Shortly after she left, two men walked up and pulled some chairs up to their table, putting Thyra and Johnathen instantly on edge. They were both wearing black leather cut off jackets with patches all over, and both sported long beards.

Isabell chirped and smiled at the two larger men. "Good to see you two again, what's been going on?"

"Just the same old shit," The bigger man said and turned his attention to Johnathen. "You don't happen to be the one that sacked that old cult member, do ya?"

"I think he is," said the red bearded man. "News said somethin' about a guy married to the gryphon and I reckon he's the only one round these parts."

Johnathen swallowed and cleared his throat, trying to not appear nervous even though he was frightened by their presence. What were they looking to do? "If you mean the gentlemen from the church, then yes, I am." Suddenly, the two fellows broke from their hardened exterior and burst into grins. The bigger man slapped Johnathen on the back. "I like this one! Good on ya boy!"

The red-bearded man slammed his hand down on the table. "It's about time one of those bastards got a good ol' ass whoopin'! They have ruined this town, ya know?"

The two men let out a course laugh and Johnathen didn't know what to say as they called over to the waitress to get her attention. Johnathen flashed the two gryphonesses an uneasy smile. They both shrugged their wing shoulders, just as confused as he was. The waitress walked over as the guys stopped their cackling and leaned against the booth.

"Alright, tweedle dumb and tweedle dumber. I heard ya. What'll it be?"

"Put his and his ladies drink on my tab. Then bring us a pitcher." The larger man exclaimed as the other man opened his cigarette pack to grab another smoke. She left once again without so much as a head nod, leaving the new party to their own devices.

The larger man looked over to the confused couple, realizing they were totally lost. "Pardon me. We didn't introduce ourselves properly. I'm Saul, and these here's my bud, Carl." Carl simply waved as Saul reached out his large, rugged hand towards Johnathen.

Johnathen reached out and shook Saul's large hand, squeezing tightly. "Nice to meet you, Saul. I'm Johnathen and this is my wife, Thyra."

Saul squeezed back hard enough that Johnathen had to suppress a wince. Saul then turned to Thyra and delicately took one of her fore claws into his hand, raising them up to give a gentle kiss to her knuckles.

"A pleasure, Thyra," Saul said with a gentle voice, causing the bird's cream cheek feathers to turn a bit red. Johnathen raised an eyebrow, not sure what to make of the man's sudden formality.

"Never would've thought we'd have another one of your kind around these parts. Hell, Isabell was the only gryphon I've met in person, until tonight." Saul added, sitting back in his chair and taking a cigarette from Carl. "It's very much welcomed, let me assure you. I enjoy her company."

Isabell gave him a beak grin and raised her mug as the

waitress arrived with the pitcher. "I can't say the same about you fat bastards, but I appreciate the compliment."

Everyone had a good laugh and poured a pint. It was quiet for a minute before Saul gestured towards the window. "I see you're a car guy, Johnathen. Is that a real Mach-1?"

Johnathen beamed ear to ear, finally finding something in common with the bikers. Isabell and Thyra listened to them ramble on about cars for a couple minutes before Isabell turned and faced Thyra, clearly bored of the men's conversation.

"So! How was the court date? I assume it went well, seeing how you all are here." Isabell casually drank from her mug while the men carried on in conversations.

"It went really well, actually." Thyra said, checking to see if Johnathen was going to chime in, but he was much too busy with his conversation. "No charges were filled, his record is clean, and he just has to pay the hospital bill." She finished off her beer and grabbed the pitcher to pour herself another. "But, there's this guy, Matthew; he's sort of the leader of the cult. He was not happy with the ruling. Johnathen said that Matthew was staring him down at the conclusion of the court day."

Isabell raised an eye ridge. "The guy sounds like a real piece of work. You all worried?"

Thyra gave a shrug. "A little bit. That man is nothing else but driven. I don't know what he plans on doing next, but it can't be good."

Isabell also finished off her beer and called over the waitress for another pitcher. "If he tries anything too dicey, know that we got your back." Thyra smiled at her new friend. "Thanks. We need all the help we can get."

Saul's speech was beginning to slur slightly from his consumption of alcohol, but he remained steadfast and sitting upright in this chair. "I just don't understand those people. Why do they constantly rag on you and your woman?"

"Because they hate gryphons and don't want them to be a part of us." Johnathen snorted, a bit woozy-headed himself. "But it's not just gryphons they hate. They hate anyone who doesn't fit their idea of what's normal. It's not a real church. It's a damned racist cult that disguises themselves as a church."

Saul dragged on the cigarette again and put it out in the ashtray. "Well, you did good by punching that one in the face, especially after how he talked to her. No one, and I mean no one, should ever talk to a lady like that. I would have whooped the ever-living dog shit out of that man."

With that, Saul downed his beer, some of it spilling into his long beard, and slammed his empty mug on the table. Carl gave him a nudge and pointed over to a small group of similar dressed men heading towards the door.

"Well, hell. Fellers, it's time for us to ride," Saul said to the group, slowly standing up from his chair.

"Don't let the door hit your fat ass on the way out," came another smart comment from Isabell.

Saul gave her a hearty chuckle and slapped Johnathen on the back once again, causing him to spill some beer from his mug. "'You let me know next time those bastards bother you again. Me and my crew will rough 'em up good."

With that, the two turned around and made their way towards the exit. The bar felt empty without the bikers' presence and considerably quieter. Then the sound of motorcycles starting up shook the small building.

Thyra turned to Johnathen, rousing her crest feathers. "It sounded like you two were having a good time. Did you make a new friend too?"

Johnathen grinned and finished his beer, then set it

down on the table. "I think we made a new ally."

Chapter 17 A New Plan

Matthew hung his robe on the coat rack next to the entrance to his office. Sighing loudly, he walked over to the stained glass window of the dimmed room and threw open the curtain. The morning sunlight had just broken the horizon of a large hill in the distance, casting a dim yellow light on the multi-colored hues of the autumn trees outside. Matthew sunk deep in thought, playing with the wooden trim around the window with his wrinkled fingers.

"This world is too beautiful to be tainted by the beasts and lesser people that walk among us," he whispered.

A knock echoed across the vaulted ceilings.

"Come in," Mathew called out, crossing his hands behind his back and continuing to gaze out the window into the field of trees.

A short blond-haired man walked into the room and closed the oak door behind him. He approached Matthew's desk and sat in one of the leather chairs in front of it. Looking quite relaxed in his black and white suit, the man breathed, "The congregation is having a special gathering this Wednesday. We hope to have enough support for the rally that you suggested later in the week."

Matthew turned around to face the young man, his bald head shining in the dim morning light. He sat down and placed his hands on the desk. "I am glad to hear everything is in order. Given the nature of the gathering I of course cannot join you, but I do have a priest that is willing to prepare a sermon for the congregation."

The young man nodded and pulled out a leather-bound notebook, jotting down some notes. "What of the press? Do they know what the purpose of this gathering is going to be?"

"Why should it matter what they know?" Matthew asked.

The blond man shrugged. "Some would frown upon this sort of display."

Matthew sat in his chair and leaned back, steepling his fingers together in front of him. He stared at the ceiling for a moment before responding.

"I doubt there will be many against us. Most of this town listens to everything I say. Even the majority of the press and police are dedicated members of the church. Any dissenters can easily be bought off." He continued gazing at the ceiling, his eyes lingering on the large wooden beams that ran along the roofline.

"As for announcing the purpose of the gathering, I will prepare a speech at the next service. Perhaps something about how this town has fallen too deeply into sin, or how we have strayed from God's light. In the end, they will believe anything I tell them." The young man gave a polite smile and jotted down some more notes as Matthew talked. After a minute, he shut the binder and placed it on his lap. "It seems you have it all under control."

"Of course, I have. Everything is under my control," Mathew retorted and let out a chuckle. He sat up straight in his chair, now paying full attention to the man sitting in front of him. "Some of the congregation has different views than others, but I think we all have the same goal in mind. A perfect world. Be it built by conversion or forceful eradication of all lesser beings, the goal is the same. I find that most have a hard time jumping to extremes, but after being prodded gently in the right direction for a time, they find themselves at that extreme without realizing it."

Matthew stood and walked over to the wall of books lining one side of the room. He idly ran his thumb across some old tomes.

"Since the dawn of man, we have desired the company of our own. Those that were different were enslaved, killed, or pushed out of the lands. It's human nature to hate others for their differences."

He pulled out a leather-bound book and opened it up, dust filling the air while he flipped through the pages. "Ancient Egypt, Jerusalem, the Romans, Germany. All of them with one goal in mind."

The book slammed shut with a loud clap before he returned it to the proper spot on the shelf. "A utopia."

Matthew walked around the room, his back hunched over as he gazed at the pictures and other old relics hanging on his wall from times of old. His footsteps were light, his hands behind his waist. His memory was like a steel trap. He could recite just about anything from the hundreds of textbooks organized perfectly on the shelves around the room. Often enough, he would, just to impress his visitors.

"Unfortunately, our modern world will not allow us to be as savage and straightforward as those in brighter days." He sneered. "No, we must be 'civilized' and 'tolerant' of others. We must learn to coexist, they say. Even when history tells us that it is not possible for us to do. They think we should evolve and that we would become better for it, but they are too blind to see what is so humanly fundamental. Understanding this, we must be smart with how we go about our work. Make them come to realize this truth without scaring them off."

The sun continued to rise as its light poured into the room. Matthew walked over to his desk and sat down once more. Taking a deep breath, he pulled out his binder. "It's hard work, but I believe it will pay off."

"Yes, Bishop. In time, we will have a population that will be willing to do anything for you," the young man stated before standing up to take his leave. He gave the man a grim smile. "Until then, you have plenty of sheep."

Matthew nodded. "Now it's time to turn them into wolves."

Chapter 18 Training day

Thyra stretched out on the carpet, arching her back and extending her foreclaws out in front of her. Her broad wings unfolded, trembling as she stretched them, her primary finger-like feathers arching towards the ceiling.

The warm, dull glow of morning sun creeped in through the edges of the curtains, adding a little light to the bedroom. Johnathen snored away with the comforter pulled up over his head.

Thyra walked into the bathroom, her talons clicking against the tile, and headed towards the scale. She had bought the large piece of equipment weeks ago to keep track of her progress, and it had become part of her daily routine to weigh every morning. "One thirty. Well, that makes three pounds lost this week."

Nutrition and BMI indexes were just starting to become available for gryphons, but with the diversity of the species, it was hard to come up with a good average weight to height ratio. The gryphon species came in all sorts of shapes and sizes, from smaller breeds with bodies the size of a house cat to breeds with bodies big as a full-grown lion. According to her own personal trainer, she was about at an ideal 'fit' weight. It had not been easy trying to shed of the pounds, but she accomplished the goals well.

She looked over at her new team uniform that hung from the door. The green and blue spandex uniform showed her team symbol and her number, thirteen. She was already getting excited for the day, and also a bit nervous. It would be her first real training day at the stadium, and she would finally get to meet all her teammates.

With a skip in her step, she took the suit off the hanger, and sat back on her haunches, stretching the fabric up over her head and crest feathers. It was a very thin and flexible material, constricting her and ruffling feathers quite annoyingly as she struggled to put it on. After a bit of cursing under her breath and falling on her back once, she had the whole outfit on.

Thyra could not help but pose in front of the mirror, checking out the large team name on her chest, and preened at some troublesome feathers. The suit was quite tight around her chest and waist, but was open to her wings, allowing for plenty of movement. Just to be certain, she halfway opened and closed her wings multiple times, testing to see if there was any restriction but found it to be top quality

"Leaving soon?" Came Johnathen's groggy voice from the bedroom, causing Thyra to chirp and exit the bathroom quickly. She walked into the room and struck a proud pose, showing off for him.

"So, what do you think?" she asked.

A grin appeared across his face. "Stunning. No wonder it took them hours to measure your body. It fits perfectly."

Johnathen lay on his side, watching her prance around and check herself out in the bedroom mirror. Her tail twitched with excitement, flicking this way and that. She turned and saw the clock on the nightstand, realizing she did not have much time left.

"Skies! I'll have to eat on the wing." Thyra leaned in and bumped her beak up against Johnathen's face, letting out a pleasant trill.

"How long is the flight to Athens? Usually takes an hour and a half by car." Johnathen asked curiously.

"I've made the flight in just about an hour before, but it's been years since I've been there."

Johnathen nodded and smiled. "Good luck today. Keep me posted."

Thyra gave him a nod and quickly left the bedroom, heading for the brightly lit kitchen. She approached the counter and looked at the banana sitting next to her satchel.

"Make sure to eat the banana on your flight. They are good for you." Johnathen shouted from the bedroom.

Her beak frowned with distaste looking at the yellow fruit. "But..."

"I don't want to hear it! You made me eat that raw pork for breakfast the other day!" Johnathen shouted back.

Thyra sighed and placed the banana in her satchel. "Fair enough!" She headed down the hallway and out the front door onto the porch.

The morning air was cool and crisp. Thyra took in a deep breath, filling her lungs with the refreshing aroma of autumn. With a quick sprint and a powerful beat of her wings, she was soon high in the sky. The flight to the stadium would give her a little time to collect her thoughts.

The scattered houses of the suburbs soon turned into the bustle of the city. She peeled back the banana peel and looked down at the fruit in disgust, taking a quick bite before swallowing it whole. Her feathers roused and her face soured up at the revolting taste.

"Ugh! How can people eat these things?" She took another couple bites, finishing off as quickly as possible and dropped the peel. "But it's so good for you, Thyra." She said, mocking Johnathen's voice almost perfectly.

As she left the city, the buildings and grays of

concrete faded into the distance. Highways and bustling cars turned into curves of thin asphalt with scattered vehicles. Warm hues of orange and yellow showed up in spots along the rolling hills. Houses became scarce as she flew further out, only occasionally obstructing the tree line.

The sun climbed higher in the sky as she flew on pure instinct. Soon, there was nothing but nature. Water beaded up on her almond brown wing feathers, rolling off easily while she beat her wings every so often to maintain altitude.

She always was happiest in the sky; it was therapeutic. Time seemed to melt away with every wing beat. Her mind clouded over in an almost dream state, and soon the only thing she heard was the beating of her wings, and the sound of wind rushing past her face. All the troubles and thoughts slipped away; she was at peace.

Then, out of the corner of her eye, she saw an object on the distant horizon. She quickly snapped out of her daze and turned her head to get a better look, instantly recognizing the shape.

It was another gryphon.

There was no doubt about it. No bird was that large. A greeting cry reached Thyra's ear tufts, and her heart started beating faster in her chest. Her wings curved upwards, crimson tail feathers fanned and raised towards the sky to quickly slow her momentum.

Thyra's beak edges curved into a grin before she breathed in deeply to let out a hawk screech in response. Her wings beat hard as she hovered in place, watching the figure grow larger and more defined. The gryphon's cere was bright yellow, and its head was decorated with deep browns. Its wingbow had a burnt orange coloration, following out to the dark brown primary feathers. He was wearing the same uniform that she was.

"Hello there!" Came the hardy voice of the equally-excited gryphon.

Thyra could tell by this point he was a male and about the same size as she was. This new Harris Hawk gryphon gave his wings a firm backstroke and began to hover in place in front of her.

"Ah! You must be the new teammate! It is a pleasure, madam," the gryphon exclaimed, having to yell over their heavy wing beats. Even with his yelling, Thyra could hear a slight accent in his voice.

"Same! Let's talk on wing," Thyra suggested.

Hovering in place not only took a lot of energy, but also was an awkward way to carry on a conversation. The male gryphon gave her a nod before suddenly folding in his wings. He leaned backwards, dropping like a stone out of the sky, rapidly descending towards the ground and rolling before flinging his wings open into a controlled glide.

He did it as if the motion was completely natural. She blinked at his effortless in such a difficult maneuver, and instantly judged his flight skill to be greater than her own. Instead of attempting the same feat, Thyra beat her wings hard and alighted herself straight before descending carefully to follow him. No use in trying to show off and risk spraining a wing on day one.

"I am Antonio, foreword left," he said as she came near. "May I ask your name?"

His voice was a lot easier to hear as she flew next to him, his primary wingtips almost touching her own. He spoke with finesse and despite the roughness in his voice, had a smooth tone to his Spanish accent.

"I'm Thyra, and I don't know my position quite yet," she replied.

Antonio looked over to her with a raised eye ridge, confused as to the gryphoness' answer. "No? You have to excuse me, but how you do not know your own position?"

Thyra almost dropped out of the air in embarrassment. Her nares flushed red, and she looked forward to avoid eye contact. She finally answered after some seconds of composing herself. "They haven't told me yet, but I was thinking about also being a forward."

Antonio raised an eye ridge, looking over at Thyra in a confused manner. "Again, pardon my rudeness, but is this your first team?"

"Actually, I've never played gryphball professionally before," Thyra admitted with another powerful wing stroke. Antonio looked away now, shocked and surprised by this news.

"I've dreamed of playing since I was a hatchling," she assured him, seeing the look in his eyes. "There were only a few teams back then, and it was such a new sport that it wasn't televised as much as it is now, but I still watched every game that I could."

Antonio saw the fire that burned in her eyes and seemed to understand her desire and passion for the game. "I do not know why an amateur was selected for this team, but someone must have seen the potential you hold. Spirit is what makes a good player. Not skill. This game is about soul and heart." Antonio told the unsure gryphoness.

Much of her discomfort lifted as she saw the kind-hearted nature in his face. She had worried that the others would laugh and tell her that she had no place in playing professionally, but at least Antonio would not. "Thank you."

The sun broke free of the morning clouds, shining brightly and causing Thyra to squint her eyes. The forest was beginning to turn into concrete once more, and in the distance she could make out the stadium, light reflecting off of the curved sides of the building.

"Ooh," she sighed.

Antonio chuckled. "A beautiful sight, no? She may not be the biggest stadium, but she is gorgeous to me."

With that, he began his decent, flying lower towards the city of Athens. The windows on the tall buildings shimmered as the gryphons flew by, gliding between them. Thyra looked down at the cars that drove beneath them, traveling about and honking at each other in the morning rush hour. The sidewalks were crowded with people, all heading towards their destinations, and some sat outside of coffee shops, talking on their phones.

Thyra followed Antonio as he seemed to know the best route through the city's labyrinth. He looked back and grinned before suddenly flapping his wings hard, speeding off. She screeched out playfully and picked up the pace herself.

His tail feathers angled and flicked, helping direct him through the twists and turns. Thyra followed close behind. She did not have to struggle, finding it easy to keep up with him. Maybe he was a better flier, but it seemed she was faster. Whether or not he was giving it his all was unknown, but it was good fun nonetheless. It had been ages since she had flown with another gryphon.

As they approached the stadium, the towering buildings became scarce, allowing for more movement between them, and Thyra saw an opening. She dove quickly and beat her wings hard, putting herself under the other gryphon in a matter of seconds. It was at that time she realized her wings were longer and broader than his, and that gave her a straight-line speed advantage.

Antonio looked behind him, eyes widening as she was nowhere to be found. She sped ahead, and her tail tuft slapped against his face as she peered up from underneath him, laughing loudly in victory. Antonio grinned and slowed his wing beats as they both dove, heading towards the front entrance of the stadium.

She landed hard on the ground, heart beating fast in her chest. Her breath was slightly labored from the short exertion and the long flight. Antonio landed beside her, folding in his wings and letting out a warm chuckle. "It seems I have been bested."

His smooth voice almost trilled, the accent even stronger than before now that they were on the earth. Thyra's tail twitched as she nodded and walked with Antonio towards the front entrance.

Thyra puffed up her cream chest feathers and pranced proudly, full of smug pride. "How does it feel being beaten by a girl?" Now that she was walking beside him, she could better judge his size. He was about the same build as she was, the burnt orange of his upper wings and body in stark contrast to the dark brown plumage that covered most of him.

He snorted. "I do not judge by the sex of another. In the human Mayan times, there were many great warriors that were female. I have no trouble admitting defeat, no matter the species or gender."

Antonio looked over at Thyra, his beak grin remaining strong. It seemed he was always smiling, no matter what was going on. He opened the door and gestured with a wing, holding it ajar for her.

"Oh, what a gentleman," Thyra mocked and stepped on inside, the polite gesture not going entirely unnoticed.

"A man should always respect a lady," he quickly retorted, following behind her.

The room opened to a wide midway, many shops and gates decorating each side of the rounded hallway. She looked around, noticing all the banners hanging from the ceiling, each depicting the Red-tails team symbol, along with an individual gryphon, name and number. She could see cutouts along the interior wall, entrances into the stands and the bright green field below. It wasn't as big as the domed gryphball stadiums in the First League, but it was still large in her eyes.

"You have never been here?" Antonio asked the curious gryphoness as she looked around. "You said you were a gryphball fan."

"Well, I am, but I mainly follow the First League teams. It's hard enough to keep up with one league, let alone two."

"Ah, that explains some things."

Thyra turned around to look at Antonio once again, surprised to see his ear tufts fold back with dismay for only a second. His energy changed quickly, ear tufts and crest feathers rousing as he smiled once again.

"Yes! There are many teams and leagues today. Hard to keep up with them all." Antonio walked past her along the long, curving hallway. The food stands on the right side had large gates shutting them off from the world and to deter thieves, or hungry gryphons, from stealing their contents inside. "So, Thyra, where is your home?"

"Macon, Georgia. Been there ever since I can remember," she replied. "Judging from your accent, you're from Mexico, or somewhere down south."

"Very good! But not quite." He nudged Thyra and laughed. Thyra almost fell over from the gryphon's nudge, and his smooth melodic voice. "Me padre is from Madrid, and mama is from Reynosa, Mexico. They adopted and raised me in San Antonio."

She felt like she could listen to him speak all day long. "So, what on earth brings you to Georgia?"

"Oh, do not mistake me! I no longer live in Texas. I

moved to Atlanta months ago-."

The sound of quick claws beating against the concrete in the distance caused both gryphons to turn their heads. They could hear heavy breathing and the clicking echoing off the rounded ceiling. They both turned to look at each other, and then behind them once again.

Either the source of the noise was far off, or it was something very small. Just as quickly as the question came to their heads, the answer came barreling around the corner. It was a lithe little gryphon, running as fast as its legs would carry it. They could see the bluish gray tint on top of its head, and big solid black eyes as it approached. The petite gryphon stopped before them and drew in a deep breath before looking up with round dark eyes.

"I'm not late, am I?!" the little gryphoness exclaimed in breathlessness, her spotted white and brown chest heaving with every gasp.

Thyra looked down at the kestrel gryphoness. She had never seen a member of her race this small in person before and wanted nothing more than to squeal with delight and pick up the housecat-sized bird, but kept herself restrained.

"Nonsense! Quite the opposite, actually," Antonio said, reassuring the tiny exhausted gryphon.

She let out a sigh and collapsed on her side, staring up at the ceiling for a moment. The black streaks around her eyes contrasted the white plumage of her face and she started to laugh. "Oh, good heavens! I thought I was going to be doomed from the start!"

She caught her breath and just as quick as she had fallen over, she was on her feet again. Thyra and Antonio flinched at the little gryphons incredibly quick movements.

"Sorry! Sorry! How rude of me. Rachel's the name!" She sat down on her haunches, her head quickly turning from one angle to the next as she seemed to study them. Rachel extended a small foreclaw, offering them handshakes in a polite introduction.

She wore the same green and blue suit that Thyra and Antonio wore, but it was so small that it seemed to be made for a baby doll. Thyra sat down, towering over her and extended a single talon for Rachel to shake.

Thyra's beak parted, bearing a big goofy grin as she could not keep herself contained any longer. "I'm Thyra! And you are the cutest little thing I have ever seen!"

The yellow cere on Rachel turned a bright shade of red and feathers roused at the compliment. "T...Thank you very much!"

Antonio stuck out a single talon as well, letting the gryphoness wrap her talons around it. "It is a pleasure, madam. I am Antonio."

She shook his talon quickly and returned to a standing position. Her tiny wings unfolding and refolding back multiple times. "A Spanish bird! Very cool! Never met one before. Well, never met many birds before. By that I mean I haven't met many gryphons, but of course I have met many birds. I mean birds are everywhere! Just the other day I ran into a rude crow and he was like, 'Hey baby, got any popcorn?' Of course, I didn't have any popcorn, so I told him no, but he didn't want popcorn, he just wanted to flirt and annoy me. He called his buddies to help annoy me, but I eventually lost him. You know, quick wings and wit can get ya far!"

Both Antonio and Thyra stood there wide-eyed, not knowing how to respond. Rachel looked at each one of them again and roused her feathers once again. "Oh heavens me, I got sidetracked again! Terribly sorry. So . . . do you know where we're supposed to be meeting, teammates?"

Alexander Bizzell

Chapter 19 Assessment

Thyra stood frozen in the entrance of the briefing room, beak open in disbelief. "I've never seen so many of us in one place."

"It is certainty exciting, is it not?" Antonio stated as he walked in behind her and sat down.

The gryphons chatted amongst themselves, some introducing themselves to others for the first time, while others looked like they had known one another for some time. They came in all colors and sizes, ranging from exotic to common avian variety. Thyra made eye contact with some of them and immediately felt out of place. These gryphons were professionals, and she was a new comer without any experience to show.

Rachel was by far the smallest of the gryphons in the room. She gulped nervously and jumped up on top of Thyra's back, finding herself more comfortable with the elevated view. "What do we do?" she asked.

Thyra twitched and looked back at Rachel in surprise but did not mind it all that much. In fact, she quite enjoyed having the pygmy gryphoness safe on her back. Thyra shared a look of uncertainty with her before heading towards the corner of the room. "I think I'll just stand over here for now."

Antonio followed, and the small party separated themselves from the busy squawks and chirping of the other gryphons in the room. A couple gryphons saw the newcomers and started to head towards them, but then the room became very quiet. Everyone turned their attentions towards the front of the room as an enormous gryphon walked in through a side door.

His facial feathers were dark gray, though most of his body was the same shade of blue as light denim, and he sported crest feathers that stood up as long as Rachel's body. His black eyes glared across the room and Thyra grew giddy with excitement, recognizing this broad size and colors from anywhere.

"That's Victor Sousa!" Thyra exclaimed quietly to her two partners.

Antonio leaned over, not daring taking his eyes of the imposing gryphon standing in front of them. "Yes, he is to be the new coach for…"

"You! Red-tail, Harris. Quiet now!" Victor's voice boomed, protruding loudly through the air with such power it felt like he was yelling straight into their faces.

Both Thyra and Antonio's feathers pressed tightly in fear against their body, making them seem much smaller than they actually were. The gryphons swallowed hard and stood as still as statues while Victor stared them down with cold, dark eyes. It made him all the more threatening. His gaze finally broke from theirs, and he began pacing slowly from wall-to-wall as he addressed the team as a whole.

"Those of you who have played for me in the past know this to be true. I am not here to be your friend. I am not here to be your pal. I am here to be your coach. You're not going to like me. You may even come to loathe me, but in the end, you will thank me for it."

All was quiet in the meeting room save for the gryphon's booming voice and sounds of his talons against the hardwood floor. None of the other gryphons dared to move. Thyra could barely breathe.

The Gryphon Generation

"Today's test will separate the wheat from the chaff. I have no room on my team for losers and weaklings. Those of you who fail today will be sent home without a second thought. For this year, I will bring this team to the first league! We will win, and we will succeed!"

Victor stopped and turned his whole body to face the group of gryphons in front of him. "Do I make myself clear?"

"Yes sir!" the group shouted in unison, their backs ramrod straight.

A faint grin appeared along his viciously curved gray beak before he turned and headed towards the exit on the far side of the room. "Good. No time to waste. Everyone, follow me."

Some of the gryphons stood up and followed Victor out immediately, while others took more time to regain their thoughts and make their limbs move once again.

"Does he really mean to fire us if we don't pass?" A pure black gryphon questioned Thyra as she brushed passed him.

"I really don't know," Thyra replied.

He swallowed and fluffed up his feathers with worry before following along closely. One gryphon at the front of the group began to laugh and turned his head to look at the black gryphon.

"If you doubt yourself, go ahead and leave. We don't need you." His white beak shone in the hallway light as they headed towards the field. His cere was bright yellow, his eyes just as dark and cold as Victors. He puffed up his chocolate-colored chest feathers, streaks of white showing up in contrast, and resettled his wings.

Thyra sent a striking glare at the gryphon, catching his eyes with her own, "Listen, he has a right to be here just as much as any of us."

Her icy reply did not seem to faze him. "Oh? And what makes you so sure? I have yet to see his worth or even more so, yours," the chocolate-colored gryphon retorted. He turned his head for a second, spying Rachel sitting up on Thyra's back. "What do we have here? A Kestrel? In the gryphon league? I hope you have a death wish, little one."

"Little one?! I'll show you who's the-the little one here when I clobber you into the earth! You...You... cloaca licker!" Every feather on Rachel's body was sticking straight up, looking more like a duster than an actual threat.

The rude gryphon laughed at her retort. "What spunk! You know, I've changed my mind. I like you. Let's hope you bring that fighting raptor spirit to the field, Miss..."

"Rachel!"

"Very good. I am Nathaniel, or Nate for short. Figured all of you should know the name of the one who will best you." He laughed once again and picked up the pace, flicking his long tail with amusement, leaving the small band to steam amongst themselves.

Rachel ground her tiny beak. "That dirty caracara! I'll pluck those tail feathers right out of his butt when I get the chance! Calling me little. I'll show him! The last time-."

"Rachel. Do not let him get the best of you. Show him what you are worth. Not with words, but with skill and spirit." Antonio was walking beside the two gryphonesses and his soothing voice and tempered mindset kept the two hotheads down from losing their cool.

Nevertheless, both of them moved forward with riled feathers, not settling down until they stepped onto the field outside. The sun was high in the sky and cast warming rays down on the grass and their plumage. The stands rose all around the round field, towering over the gryphons as the large group followed their coach out into the middle of the field.

The Gryphon Generation

Victor stood and waited for the gryphons to gather around and give him their full attention. "This test may seem very simple, but it will evaluate many aspects about each individual." He opened a broad wing that was easily the size of Thyra's entire body and used it to point towards the upper seats of the stadium. "Those devices are called Speed Falcon Threes. I have them posted around the perimeter, fifteen of them to be exact."

Thyra saw many long cylinders mounted on podiums all around the interior. These devices were decorated with cameras and sensors that moved independently, giving a good indication that they were autonomous.

"I will call upon you lot one at a time," he continued. "You are to fly around the perimeter of the field and get within range of the canons. Once you are in range they will fire a gryphball every three seconds. The goal is to catch every ball fired from them. If you let one ball hit you, you will be eliminated."

Whispers formed between the gryphons as they talked amongst themselves, mostly in worry. Victor let them chat for just a couple seconds before speaking up once again.

"Points will be awarded for every ball caught. Double the points will be lost for every ball missed. If you fumble a gryphball, you will be eliminated. I have no room on this team for a bird that can't catch. You must hold the ball for the three seconds before the next one is fired. Only then will you drop the ball."

The crowd mumbled amongst each other again. Victor sent a warning glare at them and took a deep breath. "Any questions?"

Not a soul made a sound.

"Good. We will begin immediately." His cold black eyes looked directly over to Antonio. "You, Harris, you're up first."

Antonio took a deep breath and nodded. The brown and burnt orange gryphon slowly stood and walked past the group. "Wish me luck."

With Antonio next to him Victor seemed even larger than before, standing a good foot taller than the smaller bird. "Everyone, back to the dugout. Clear the field and take notes on Antonio's performance."

The group turned tail and walked over to the edge of the field, leaving the two in the middle. Antonio looked up at Victor, confused as to how he knew his name. The gigantic gryphon simply watched the others leave, not looking at him once.

"You don't think I've done my homework? I know everything about you and the rest of them too. I know where you come from, your previous experience, and what you had for dinner last night." Victor's gray crest feathers fanned out, looking even larger than before and he turned his head, looking down at the smaller gryphon at his side. "I expect you to give a good performance. You used to be one of the greats, until your accident. Let's hope today is your day."

The great gryphon now left Antonio, walking slowly towards the dugout. Antonio was shocked, standing frozen, his eyes wide at the mention of his accident.

Flashes of screaming from thousands of people filled his mind. He saw the sky, the stadium and the ground all at once as he plummeted quickly towards the earth. Antonio shivered, wings settling and twitching as he relived the memory once more. A pain shot through his wing and he winced, looking over at the scar that covered his wing shoulder.

"Harris! Are you ready?" Victor called out from the sidelines, pulling Antonio back to reality.

Antonio took a deep breath and widened his stance, crouching like a tiger about to pounce on its prey. "Ready!"

"Begin!"

Antonio pushed off of the earth with all his might, copper wings raising and pulling down in one powerful motion, sending the gryphon high in the air. Victor gave a nod at the display of power and Antonio's worry faded as he climbed higher into the sky.

Then there was a loud bang and one of the launchers threw a white gryphball at Antonio with mind-boggling speed. His brown eyes quickly moved and focused on the white hurtling at him. With a smooth wing beat, he aligned himself towards the ball and pulled it against his chest. He grunted as it hit him with great force, almost knocking the wind out of him, but he did not falter. Antonio tucked one wing and rolled, diving once again to gain speed. After three seconds, he dropped the ball

He heard another shot from the opposite end of the field. This time, the ball was thrown way short. With a powerful wing beat, he dove underneath the falling orb and caught it before it hit the ground. His wings spread open, carrying momentum upwards, and he began to circle around the inner perimeter of the stadium. Every three seconds he dropped the current ball and tilted his ear tufts towards the sound of another projectile being launched.

Thyra and Rachel watched in awe as he flew from end to end with blistering speed. It was like watching a bat at dusk, flying wildly around catching bugs. His wings curved and snapped out with incredible precision as he caught every ball that was fired at him.

Victor stood quietly, clicking a counter he held in his talons. Finally, a timer beeped loudly, signaling the end of Antonio's test. "Time!" the coach bellowed at the exhausted gryphon.

Antonio dove and came in towards the dugout in a smooth glide. He landed softly and stood straight while the gryphons rose up in a cheer, chirping and squawking praise. Antonio's chest heaved quickly, short of breath, but he held his head high, a pleased grin appearing on that black and yellow beak.

He gave bowed to them and walked over to the shocked gryphonesses, who standing there with dumbfounded smiles. "A perfect score. Twenty out of twenty."

Victor walked out from the group and turned to look directly into Antonio's eyes. "Good job. Very good job. These gryphons will be lucky to have you on the team." He turned his attention to the rest of them. "I hope you lot took notes of his incredible performance! This is what I expect from my team. Precision. Control. Speed. Both on and off the ground."

Antonio roused his feathers with pleasure and gave another bow, touching the grass with his curved beak tip. "Thank you, Coach."

"Now who will volunteer to go next?"

Everyone was dead silent once again. Victor looked over the multi colored gryphons, waiting for someone to come forward.

Thyra took a deep breath and raised her wing. "I'll do it."

The other gryphons stepped to the side to make way for her. She could feel the many avian eyes watching, some judging her while others were just thankful she volunteered instead of Victor barking at them to go.

The coach nodded and followed Thyra out to the middle of the field. As he did so, Victor spoke to her almost in a whisper, "Keep your chin up. Make sure to follow each ball and when it hits, hold on tight."

Thyra was surprised by this sudden new side of the coach. Earlier it hadn't seemed like he cared who would mess up. "Why are you giving me advice?"

He did not look down at her, simply walking beside her until they were in the middle of the field. "Because unlike all the others, you haven't played a single game of gryphball before. Now I don't know why you were sent to me, but Richard saw something in you. I intend to find out what that was."

He continued to speak quietly, motioning to the different cannons lining the perimeter as if he was explaining the machines to her and how they worked. "I doubt you'll be able to catch every ball, but make sure you hold each one you do catch. The canons are quite powerful, and no matter what Richard thinks I will have to stick to my word if you fumble one by accident. Do I make myself clear?"

Thyra swallowed down her fear and gave him a confident nod. Victor turned tail quickly and began walking back towards the dugout.

"Good."

Time seemed to slow down for her, every step he took feeling like it lasted for several seconds. Thyra closed her eyes for a second, concentrating on the goal. She could hear the air pulling into her lungs, feel the sun's rays being absorbed into her feathers, and the feeling of the grass under her talons.

She needed to go about this smartly. If the canons were powerful, then she needed to fly towards the center of the field. It would give her more time to react and the balls wouldn't hit her as hard once they had lost their momentum.

The conversation with Antonio came back to her memory. *All about spirit.*

"Thyra! Are you ready?" Victor called out from the edge of the field, causing Thyra to snap her eyes open.

Her green avian orbs burned bright with new

determination. "Let's do it."

Chapter 20 Resistance

The doorbell chimed away and yet another person entered the cramped coffee shop. Soft jazz music played over the radio near the counter as a long-haired man prepared a cup of coffee for the new customer. Isabell watched from a corner booth with a coffee cup in her talons and took in a deep breath of her coffee, inhaling the aroma of ground beans wafting from her cup.

Having a long and slender beak made drinking from normal cups difficult, especially when it was hot liquid, but she made it work without spilling it on herself. She wore a plain black gryphon cut t-shirt with a band name on the front. The silver piercings in her ear tufts and cere reflected the dim, warm light in the small shop.

Her phone buzzed loudly on the wooden table in front of her, causing the glass container of sugar to shake. She picked up the device, adorned with charms and fake jewels, and scrolled through the message. It was a news link from the biker, Saul, which was odd. Usually he just sent a "what's up?" or asked why she wasn't at the bar.

She opened the link and started to read through the article. The more she read, the angrier she got. She ground her beak, clicking loudly while her feathers puffed up.

The coffee shop attendant chose that moment to walk over to Isabell to top off her water. He looked once at her and immediately saw that she was disgruntled. Gryphons were very expressive with their body language, and someone knew what to look for, it was hard for them to hide their emotions.

"Hey Isabell. You all good?" the barista asked, putting down the water pitcher on the table.

She closed her eyes and took a deep breath, settling her feathers down for a moment. "Yeah, Paul, all good." She put down the phone and picked up the coffee once again, taking a sip.

Paul stood there for a minute and then sat down at the table. "Cause you had that thing going on again, with the feathers. Usually that's like not a good sign. Wanna talk about it?"

He reached into his apron and pulled out a pack of cigarettes, offering one to the clearly upset bird. She gave him a grateful look and took one between her talons. He quickly brought out a lighter, flicking it open and striking it. She leaned in and took a puff, blowing a thick cloud of smoke into the air.

"Make this an Irish coffee," Isabell said and sat back in her booth, resettling her violet and black wings.

Paul chuckled and made his way behind the bar, coming back with a bottle of Irish liquor while puffing on a cigarette himself. He popped the top off and poured a good amount into the black brew, turning it a light shade of brown.

Isabell took another drag of her smoke and picked up the now heavily liquored coffee. "It's these goddamn fascists."

Paul leaned back in his chair and gave her a nod, playing with his dreadlocks. "Yeah. Seems like they're everywhere, man."

"And they aren't going anywhere for a while," she said with a sigh, taking a large drink of the hot brew. She settled her wings and looked over at Paul. "This article I was just reading is about an anti-gryphon rally being organized, but the news is disguising it as a church picnic. It's sickening!"

"Yeah man, it is."

"Even worse, it's in Thyra's hometown."

Paul squinted and took another puff from his cigarette, clearly lost. "Thyra..?"

Isabell stared at Paul. "The gryphoness I told you about?"

"Oh yeah, man. That's right. She sounded cool," Paul said with a smile, clearly lost as to what his part was supposed to be in the conversation.

Isabell could only laugh, knowing he meant well, even if he was not the brightest. "She is, but I just feel shitty about her having to deal with that oppression."

"Yeah that's definitely not cool. People need to like, learn to like everyone."

Isabell thought for a minute, taking another swig of the coffee. Her short ear tufts perked up with an idea. "You know what, Paul? We should go to this 'picnic' and show them they are wrong. Show them that we will not tolerate racism or speciesism."

Paul nodded with agreement. "A good ol' fashioned protest, huh? I like it. Haven't been in once since last year."

Isabell put out the cigarette butt in the ashtray and finished up the alcoholic coffee with one last swallow. The gryphoness collect her things and threw a couple dollars down on the table, then slid out of the booth and stood next to Paul.

"You think you can gather up a group by Wednesday?"

Paul squinted his eyes again and put out his own cigarette butt, then stood up, rubbing the back of his head. "Um...What's today?"

Isabell sighed and gave Paul a dirty look. "Monday."

"Oh! Then, yeah. Totally. I'll get a group and make up some gnarly signs too."

Isabell gave his arm a playful smack with her tail while walking away. Paul grabbed at his arm in fake pain, then laughed. "Ouch, dude."

"See you Wednesday morning, then," she said and went outside.

Bright rays of light in the autumn morning caused her deep blue eyes to squint. Her phone vibrated in the purse she wore around her neck, and she pulled it out to check the new message.

Meet at the bar tonight.

"Saul must have an idea," Isabell mumbled. She locked the screen and threw the device back into her purse.

The cool air suddenly picked up, ruffling her violet black feathers. Isabell put her foreclaws out in front of her and stretched her back out, much like a cat would, unfolding her wings in the process. With her eyes now adjusted, she looked around the small parking lot for the coffee shop. It was mostly empty save for a couple of old pickup trucks, most likely left over from the night before. She leaped forward into a sprint, and her short wings snapped open, giving a firm flap to bring her airborne.

&❧

Thyra collapsed onto the cool grass on the edge of the field. Another gryphon was up in the air, curving this way and that as he ran the course. Tiny Rachel sat next to the exhausted gryphoness, holding a water bottle. As she waited for Thyra to catch her breath again, she talked nonstop.

"Fourteen out of twenty is not the worst score, but it isn't the best either! I've seen some pretty bad tests in my day. The last team I was on, there was this pelican gryphon, I don't know why he was trying to make the team in the first place, but this pelican thought he could play. You should have seen him flapping around and trying to corner! His giant beak made it so hard for him to see and to turn and he only caught two! And then-."

"Rachel!" Antonio warned, looking down at the twitchy little gryphoness. She chuckled and offered the bottle of water to Thyra, who took it and emptied it within seconds.

"You should be happy with the performance you gave, Thyra. It was most impressive!" Antonio said and sat down, looking towards the sky as the black-and-white-striped gryphon put on a good show for the audience.

It was Nathaniel. The abrasive gryphon certainly knew how to catch the balls with style. Nevertheless, he missed the last ball. A loud screech came from his yellow and black beak as the timer buzzed out, calling the gryphon back down. He landed just as quickly as he had taken off, grinding his beak while walking towards the dugout.

Nathaniel caught sight of Thyra and her friends looking at him and screeched again at them in anger, black eyes narrowing. "What the hell are you all staring at!"

Antonio and Rachel blinked back at him, not sure what to say.

"You did very admirably Nate," Antonio began. "It was—."

"I don't need your praise!" Nate squawked, cutting him off. The hot-tempered gryphon snorted through his nares and stomped off, cursing in bird speech under his breath.

"Caracaras. Always the same," said a female voice.

All of them turned to look at the speaker, a new

gryphoness who was approaching them. She stood a good deal larger than Antonio, almost as large as the coach. Her striking yellow eyes were surrounded by red circles and her face was white except for a black patch that ran under her eyes and hung down like a beard from her beak.

She sat with the group, and her curved beak gave them a warm smile. Her voice was kind. Soft, but broken, as she muttered from word to word. "You will have to ignore Nate. He is very prideful, and extremely competitive."

Thyra sat up on her haunches, looking at the Bearded Vulture gryphoness who had joined them. "Way ahead of you. He's sort of a jackass." Thyra said rubbing her head, causing the white gryphoness to chuckle gently. She seemed to have a relaxing aura about her.

"Jackass is a good word to use. Give him time. He will warm up to you. He can make for a great teammate." She held out a heavily feathered foretalon and Thyra saw that her arms all the way up to her talons were covered in thick white feathers. "Aadhya. Good to have new faces on the team."

Thyra tried not to wince at the name. It sounded like the gryphoness was trying to cough up a hairball as she pronounced it. She reached out with her own foretalon and shook the other gryphoness' firmly. "Nice to meet you, Ad... Adha..."

Aadhya chuckled again and dropped her talon. "Most call me Addy for short."

"I'm sorry. That is a lot easier!" Thyra replied with a chuckle of her own. "I'm Thyra. This is Antonio and Rachel."

They all shared good talon shakes and smiled at the introduction. Addy's striking yellow eyes shone brightly as she looked to each one of them.

"Lammergeier, you're up next," Victor demanded, looking to Addy.

Her short crest feathers ruffled up and she stood, readjusting her peppered black and white striped wings before bowing to the group. "We can talk later. Wish me luck!"

They all nodded as Addy turned around and head towards the center of the field. Thyra chucked the bottle of water away in a garbage can and sighed, spreading her wings out a bit in irritation.

"I don't think my wings have ever been this sore! Moving around like that can really take a toll on the joints."

"It will get easier with practice," Antonio said reassuringly. His own wing was throbbing with pain right where his scar was, annoyingly reminding him of his limits. Yet he showed no discomfort in his face or body language.

They all focused on Addy, who had taken to the air and was floating like a prop plane in the sky. She seemed to soar in an almost lazy manner, but as soon as the first ball fired, she had it in her claws. She was slow but had grace about her. She drifted effortlessly, catching every ball that came near, but the gryphballs that were out of her reach, she made no extra effort to catch.

"She doesn't have to score very high because she's a defender," Antonio said, leaning in closely, his voice a near whisper.

Rachel and Thyra both nodded in understanding. Each gryphon not only possessed different skills, but their abilities varied by species. This was the reason the teams were so varied by species and why certain breeds played specific positions.

The buzzer sounded off, ending Addy's turn. She drifted down to the earth and landed without so much as an extra wing beat.

"Thirteen," Victor said, confirming her score.

She waltzed past him and nodded in acknowledgement as she made her way back to Thyra's group. They smiled and congratulated her for the efforts.

"Kestrel, you're up next!" the coach called.

Rachel puffed up and ran off before Thyra could wish her good luck. She skipped and maneuvered through the mass of birds and stood at Victor's feet, looking up confidently at the towering gryphon. "I got this in the bag coach! You'll see. I'll catch every ball! On the last course that I flew-."

"KESTREL," he barked. "To the center."

She tilted her head and quickly jumped up before darting to the center of the field, leaving Victor to rub his face with irritation. Rachel stood at the center of the field, wings twitching and settling constantly, more than ready to show off. Then Victor gave the signal and Rachel was off into the sky with vicious wing beats.

Thyra's eyes grew wide at the tiny gryphoness' speed, flying vertically just as fast as Thyra could dive. Rachel came to the center of the field, high in the air above the stadium and stopped. She seemed to float in place now, wings flapping but not moving her forward, almost like someone had her on a string.

The sound of cannon fire filled the stadium as the first ball launched, and Rachel dove with blinding speed. Thyra had been worried how the diminutive bird would handle the force of the balls, but instead of meeting it head on, Rachel followed it, carrying her momentum to match the speed of the projectile. She plucked the ball out of the air as if it was standing still, leaving Thyra shocked.

"How is she doing that?" Thyra asked.

Antonio smiled as Rachel rose up and levitated in the air once again, ready for the next ball. "Size has a lot of factors."

"That's why I'm asking! When I caught the ball, it felt like being punched in the chest! They come out with such force."

"She gains speed to match the ball and catches it that way. It is truly fascinating, no?" Antonio replied.

The group watched with amazement as Rachel darted around the stadium, plucking every ball effortlessly out of the air until the buzzer sounded once again. Within the blink of an eye, Rachel was back down on the ground right beside the coach. Her little tawny chest moved so quickly it looked like mere vibration as she caught her breath once again.

"See I told ya so! Easy peasy. Need to come up with something a bit more difficult, coach!"

Victor simply shook his head as he watched the little gryphon skip back over to the band. "Alright birds! Break for lunch. I want everyone back here at thirteen hundred hours. Dismissed."

Chapter 21 A New Plan

The cold night air pierced through Isabell's down, causing her dark feathers to fluff as she flapped her wings. She gained some altitude and glided along with the wind until she spotted the flickering neon sights of the small bar. There was a group of motorcycles and a couple cars parked outside. A slow night, but that was to be expected on a weekday. Isabell landed softly right in front of the doors where two bikers stood. One of them opened the door and gave her a polite smile.

The music was turned down low. She heard the sound of billiard balls cracking against each other. When the place was packed, it had a haze of smoke in the air like a thick morning fog, but tonight she could see across the room.

The floor was peeling up in places, and the paint on the walls was blotchy. Each worn seat in the booths was covered with patchwork repairs, and the wooden tables were ancient. This dive bar was far from elegant, but it had its charm, one that Isabell absolutely loved.

No sooner had she stepped inside than a loud voice echoed from across the bar.

"There's that bitch!"

Isabell chuckled and walked deep into the open room, passing by the billiard tables and the bikers playing before replying back, "Shut your bastard mouth, you big oaf!"

Isabell slapped her tail against Saul's broad back and hopped up into her favorite booth, sitting across from Saul.

The brute bellowed with a laugh and turned his mug upside down, finishing off the golden yellow beer. "Been well?"

Isabell nodded and brought out a pack of cigarettes. She offered one to Saul, who gratefully took it. "I'm about as good as a hen could be in this screwed up world," she said, then flicked open her silver lighter and struck the flint, producing a warm flame as she puffed on the cigarette.

Saul did the same and shook his head. "Sorry I had to break that news to you this morning."

Isabell shrugged. "It's alright. I would have found out sooner or later."

The waitress walked over, looking to Isabell as she picked up Saul's empty mug. "Hey darlin' thing. The usual?"

Isabell nodded to the waitress and returned her attention to the biker across from her. "Where's your better half?"

"Carl is working overtime at the shelter. Said something about a coworker being sick," Saul said with a shrug of his own.

The next song began to play on the jukebox, and the waitress soon returned with two icy mugs of golden beer and sat them on the table. Isabell lifted one up and clanked it against Saul's mug in a toast before taking a large drink.

She closed her eyes and sighed, feeling much better. "Nothin' like a cold one after the day's end."

The biker grinned, watching the gryphoness enjoy her beer. "One of life's only good things."

She laughed and gently put the mug on the table. Both of them sat in silence for a minute, listening to the soft old rock music and the clanking of billiard balls. Large televisions above the bar on the other side of the room played clips of the week's gryphball match.

"You said something about a plan?" Isabell finally questioned.

Saul placed his mug down softly and sat up in the booth. He leaned over the table with his hands crossed so his face was much closer to Isabell's beak. "I've already gathered over a hundred men. We estimate there to be an easy three hundred on the other side."

Isabell's short black eartufts rose. "Go on."

"Seeing how they're disguising this as a peaceful church picnic instead of a rally, police presence will be very minimal. Maybe even non-existent."

"I figured as much," she replied. "What if they get violent? We're going to be outnumbered."

Saul could not help but laugh. "Over a hundred bikers versus a couple hundred churchgoers? There won't be a fight, but even if there was, that would be a stupid decision on their part."

Isabell's feathers ruffled in displeasure at the biker's response. "Saul, you don't understand."

Saul raised an eyebrow and picked up his beer once more, taking another swig as he leaned on one arm, waiting for an explanation.

Isabell drew out another cigarette and puffed from it once more. "These people aren't just churchgoers. They want my kind dead. They hate everything about us. They see us as 'unpure beasts' and 'creatures made outside of God's natural creation.' Our very existence is a sin incarnate." She threw up a foreclaw, mocking the speeches she had heard time and time again. "These man-made beasts represent the folly of mankind. A sick disease we must eradicate!"

Isabell snorted through her nares and tilted her mug to the ceiling, downing the rest of her beer. She slammed the mug down on the table, eyes burning with anger and aggression. "Don't you get it?! People like them would burn us alive at the stake if they could have their way!"

She took a long drag of her cigarette and held it in, closing her eyes as she tried to calm down. The squawking voice of the angry gryphoness had carried far. Many eyes had focused in on the booth. Saul waited silently and sent warning glares to the onlookers. Soon enough, the clanking of billiard balls resumed once again.

Isabell looked away from him, a tear rolling down the side of her beak and falling onto the table. "Sorry. It's...It's just been a long day. I'm just tired of these cult members getting away with oppressing us openly without so much as a little resistance from anybody."

She wiped at her eyes with a wing tip and put out the cigarette butt. The waitress snuck over and quietly grabbed the mugs before sitting new, filled ones down. She took another drink and let herself calm down, trying to find words to begin the conversation once more.

With a deep breath, she met Saul's eyes once more. "We can't start a fight with them. It just takes one hit. One punch being thrown, and it's over. In the eyes of the public, we will be the bad guys. They are just having a peaceful picnic, as the news put it. If they got their hands on me they could beat me, break me to pieces and no one would do anything about it. They would just say that I was extremely aggressive, and they acted in self-defense."

Saul picked up the new mug and sipped from it, lost in thought himself. "We won't let anything happen to you or the other gryphons."

"I know you won't. Not intentionally," Isabell told the rough-looking man, giving him a faint beak grin. She drew out her cell phone from a leather pouch and looked down at the screen.

"You expecting a call?" Saul asked curiously. Isabell

nodded her head and put the cell phone away once again. "Yeah, I texted Thyra and Johnathen to see if they would join our cause tomorrow."

"Johnathen? You mean the fancy boy from last week?" Isabell nodded again to confirm Saul's question. He laughed a bit and picked up his mug, leaning back into the booth. "I wouldn't count on him. He doesn't seem like the social justice type."

"You'd be wrong! Thyra had told me that he got several laws implemented that helped gryphons, and he used to attend The Gathering when he was younger. He has insight on how they operate."

Saul raised a shaggy eyebrow, clearly intrigued by this new information. "Why didn't you tell me this earlier? Any information on The Gathering members could help us."

Isabell shrugged her wing shoulders, readjusting her short black wings. "I just didn't think about it. You said you had a plan, so I wanted to hear you out first before I brought new information to you."

"Well, call that boy up. Let's get him down here."

&⚓

Thyra resettled her almond-brown wings, wincing at the aching pain from the days exercises. Sighing, she slammed her locker shut and sat back on her haunches.

"Was a rough day, no?" Antonio wore a smile along his curved beak and sat down next to the exhausted gryphoness.

Thyra chuckled and looked over at him. "Yeah, I don't think I'm going to fly home. I'll just have to let Johnathen know I'll be staying at a hotel tonight."

Antonio tilted his head. "Johnathen?"

"Oh! He's my husband," she explained.

Rachel padded up from around the corner of the lockers, her eartufts perked in attention. "Husband? I didn't know you were married! Who is the gryphon? Maybe I know him! I know quite a lot of gryphons around here! In fact, let me guess. Is it-?"

Thyra cut into Rachel's endless bantering. "He's human."

Both Antonio and Rachel stared at Thyra for a good minute before busting out into laughter, their chirping calls making the other gryphons in the locker room turn their heads to look at the loud party.

"I wasn't aware you were a comedian, Thyra!" Antonio joked, giving her a playful little shove with a wing shoulder.

Thyra turned to face them both with glare. "What's so funny about that?"

The other two's laughter ceased.

"No way. Antonio, I think she's serious. I mean, that's unheard of. Never thought of it. I mean, I guess it could work and apparently it does! I mean, that's cool, Thyra. I just-. Sorry for laughing. I, uh . . ." Rachel hung her head, pinning her eartufts back with embarrassment. Antonio did the same.

Thyra nipped each one of them on the top of their heads and turned to fumble with the lock on her locker. "No, it's alright. I know it's a new concept but believe me. You all will meet Johnathen soon, and then you'll understand."

They both nodded and gave her embarrassed smiles before following Thyra out of the locker room. The door opened up back into the main lobby of the stadium, which looked especially eerie at night. Most of the lights were cut off, except the bare amount to lead them to the front gates.

The cool night air filled Thyra's lungs and the parking lot lights filled the sky with an artificial glow.

"I hope you enjoy your evening, Thyra. Hasta mañana," Antonio said, giving a polite bow to the two other gryphonesses before taking to the sky.

Rachel turned to Thyra. "So, are you alright for the night? I mean, I could wait here while you made reservations and made sure you had a room, or I could call someone for you because I'm in this town a lot and I do know a couple places. Chattanooga isn't that far of a flight for me, but sometimes I get lazy and just book a room here. You could try the Quick Break hotel on Main, or if you want something a little better there's this really nice place over on Central called The Resort, but it can be a little pricey!"

Thyra shook her head and smiled down at the gryphon who never stopped moving, her head darting like a hummingbird. It was nice of Rachel to care so much for her, even though they just met this morning. "I'll be fine. Thank you for the suggestions."

Rachel grinned in response and ruffled her tan feathers. "Alright! Well if you go to the resort, tell 'em the little mug sent ya. I'm sure one of 'em will know me."

With that, the little bird quickly jumped into the air and sped off like a tiny rocket, wings flapping rapidly in the night air. Within seconds, she was gone, lost in the darkness.

Thyra let out a small sigh and sat down to reach into her neck pouch. She pulled out the flip phone and hesitated, figuring Johnathen was probably asleep. Instead of calling, she decided to text. Thyra cursed at the small phone keyboard, her tired claws stumbling around the letters to try and spell out her message.

"I never understood the human obsession with text messaging," A soft voice came from behind her. Thyra took her eyes away from the screen to turn, noticing the large gryphon standing behind her. Aadhya smiled gently and sat down next to Thyra, her angel white feathers and black 'beard' bristling gently with the breeze.

"It's a necessary evil," Thyra replied. "The humans love to text, my husband being one of them."

"True." Aadhya gave her a small nod and looked up into the sky. "I heard the conversation earlier, and I give you my congratulations. It is hard in this world to find a soul mate. We may have just met, but I can say that I am happy for you. In my opinion, it matters not what species or sex one's mate is, as long as one is happy."

Thyra blinked at the great bird, surprised by the show of support. "Thank you."

"You are most welcome," she said and when Thyra went back to finishing her text, added, "Forgive my interruption, but I also heard you saying you were too tired to make the flight back home. I do not know where 'home' is, but if you would like, I have an apartment here in Athens. You may join me there, if you wish."

Thyra lowered her phone and looked back at Aadhya, stunned by the invitation. The large gryphon stood quietly, the essence around her calming. It was almost like Thyra had known this gryphoness since she was a chick. "That would be awesome."

Aadhya chuckled, turning her piercing red and yellow eyes on the smaller gryphoness. "Awesome. I enjoy this word. So informal but that seems appropriate between acquaintances. Now, are you too tired to fly the short distance to my apartment? I could call a cab if you desired."

"No. I think I can handle it. It was just the long flight I wanted to avoid," Thyra assured her, resettling her wings.

Aadhya started to walk towards the large empty parking lot. "Good. I find automobiles far too troublesome to get in and out of. Also, they are just so very slow."

The white gryphoness opened her gigantic wings and leapt into the air with a couple long lazy wing beats. Thyra quickly followed behind, and in moments they were gliding towards the city.

Thyra banked with Aadhya as they passed between two large buildings, twisting through the maze of structures. The city streetlights and cars buzzing below created a warm glow all around them as she Thyra followed along. "You get used to them, you know. Cars. Johnathen always drives us to dinner, and if you think all cars are slow, you should see his!"

"I have never been in any fast car," Aadhya admitted. "Perhaps it would be entertaining."

Aadhya turned another corner and then gently dove, floating down to the street to land without so much as a steadying wing beat. Thyra landed next to her, stirring up trash and other city debris with hard backwards wing strokes.

The apartment building was a little on the rough side, its windows and front door barred up. Aadhya walked up the stairs and reached into her satchel to bring out keys, fumbling with them for a minute before unlocking the front door. Thyra walked into the lobby, where the mailboxes and elevator were. The light inside was dim and the tan wallpaper was peeling off the walls.

Thyra followed the large gryphoness into the elevator and up to the apartment. They walked down a long hallway and Aadhya unlocked her door, swinging it open to reveal the small cramped interior. The room was decorated with various candles, tapestries, and a golden idol of an elephant with many arms at the far wall. Thyra blinked at the place.

Aadhya picked up Thyra's surprise. "It is not much, but it is a good home. I do not need many earthy possessions, and this does nicely," she assured her, hanging up her keys and satchel on hooks next to the entrance. She padded into the small kitchen, her huge body taking up the entirety of the space. Thyra walked up to the golden idol, which was adorned with many flowers and candles, curious as to its origin.

"Addy, what is this?"

Aadhya took a tea pot off of the stove and began filling it with water, looking over the counter at Thyra in the living room. "That is Ganesha, a deity among my culture."

Thyra gave a nod of acknowledgement as she curiously looked around the rest of the room, noticing paintings of other deities and also a photo of Aadhya with two humans. They both wore elaborate clothing of many colors and had darker skin. Both of them had red dots on their forehead. They were hugging Aadhya and big smiles illuminated their faces.

"So, you were born in India?"

Aadhya put the pot on the stove and turned it on. The gryphoness did not have to stand up tall to reach the cupboard above the stove, pulling out a box of tea bags." Not born. Made, yes."

Thyra looked closely at the two Indian people, one male and one female. "Are these your parents?"

"Yes. Both of them were scientists in the lab and adopted me after the experiments were complete." Aadhya took out two cups from the opposing cabinet and sat them down on the counter. "Would you like tea?"

Thyra could tell that was an emotional subject, one that she should not press especially with someone she just met today. Thyra walked over to the kitchen counter, looking over at the pot of steaming water and the tea bags. She frowned. "I've only ever had iced tea or sweet tea. Is it good hot?"

Aadhya gave her a hearty laugh and put the bags into

the now whistling teapot. She turned off the stove and sat the pot aside, looking back over to the curious gryphoness. "You mean better than the repulsive way southern Americans fill their tea with sugar? Yes. It is the original and far superior way."

Thyra beak grinned and moved over to the couch as Aadhya prepared the tea. "I take it you're traditional about your tea."

Aadhya poured the cups and took them in a foreclaw, walking over on three legs into the living room and setting both on the coffee table in front of the couch. She stepped up into the loveseat seating opposite the sofa and adjusted her large body, holding the hot cup of tea steady.

"Absolutely."

Thyra chuckled again and took the teacup that sat on the table, holding it in a foreclaw to take a deep breath of it. The beverage was dark green and smelled very different than that of sweet tea. Thyra blew gently and took a small sip; her beak turned a sour note and she scrunched her eyes.

Aadhya sipped on her tea, smiling at Thyra's reaction. "I assume it is not to your liking?"

"I guess my tongue isn't as refined as yours." Thyra put down the cup and took a deep breath. "I think it needs a bit of sugar. Actually, a *lot* of sugar."

Both gryphons laughed together for a moment and Thyra asked, "So, how long have you been playing gryphball?"

"It must be at least ten years now." Aadhya set down her cup on the small table next to the sofa and crossed her gigantic talons, visibly relaxing as she recollected the past.

"I was young, must have been at least five years old at the time, and living with my foster parents. Gryphball was just gaining popularity in India, but I was one of the biggest gryphons in the nation, and as a result, a recruiter found me quite quickly. I knew what the sport was, and both parents told me to try. I found myself on India's very first team, and I have been playing ever since."

Thyra listened to the story, sipping on her tea occasionally, forcing herself to swallow the bitter substance. She was slightly confused as to what would bring her the gryphoness all the way from India to the southern part of America. "Why go from such a large European league to something as small as the second league here?"

"I always wanted to come to America. I wanted to experience the culture and the people, but most of all, see other gryphons. I heard that the experiments were very successful over here, and the population was plentiful. I quit the league over there and came here to join the only one I could find with a defender opening." Aadhya finished her tea and sat the empty cup on the table. "I took a slight pay cut, but money is no matter to me. I am happy with my decision and hope to see our team do great things."

The great gryphon stood from the couch, ruffling her white and black feathers before making way to a small chest in the far side of the room. Aadhya grabbed a couple pillows and a large knitted blanket from the chest and handed them over to Thyra. "I hope that couch is comfortable enough, I have no other nest to offer you."

"This is more than fine! Thank you so much. Saved me quite a bit of cash and a lot of boredom"

Thyra took the blanket and pillows, and Aadhya gathered up the cups, taking them into the kitchen. She put the cups away and walked back into the living room with a smile. Thyra had already made herself comfortable with the blanket laid out across her body and her head against the soft pillow.

"The bathroom is down the hall to your right, and if

you need anything else, just ask," Aadhya said.

"Thanks."

"Rest well. We must be at the field by seven once again."

Thyra nodded and Aadhya turned off the lights and disappeared down the short hallway. The city lights showed through the thin curtain, illuminating the cozy living room in a warm glowing light. Thyra stared at the ceiling for some time, letting her mind wander.

What a long day it had been. She had met many other gryphons, more than she had met in her entire life. Their faces came back to mind as she tried to remember all their names, but tomorrow was a new day. She closed her eyes, took a deep breath, and let sleep take over.

Chapter 22 Uneasy

"Thyra...Thyra..."

The voice sounded so distant, but so close. Her eyes slowly opened, finding herself in a pure white room. Sunlight poured in from window on the far side of the wall into the room and reflected off the walls and ceiling, making it incredibly bright inside. She was sitting at a table, staring at two men dressed in lab coats, and they were much taller than her. Or had she shrunk?

"Thyra, you haven't eaten anything yet. Are you alright?" One of the men asked, pointing down to the plate set out before her.

"You must be hungry after playing with the football all day. You must eat to regain energy." The other man said, pointing at the well-used football in the corner of the room.

The steak was grilled only slightly, the center left rare and bleeding. Many green beans decorated the plate along with a large helping of mashed and buttered potatoes. Thyra opened her beak to speak, but no words came out, just a feral chirp. She clamped her beak, head rushing with thought as she tried to form the words in her mouth.

"B...belly... Hurts."

She was able to finally get it out. The words sounded unlike her own voice and felt unnatural. The two men looked at each other and began frantically scribbling down notes on clipboards.

"Fantastic! She can describe pain now," said one man

said to the other. They both nodded in approval and turned back to Thyra once again. "Do you want the pain to go away?"

Thyra tilted her head. Their voices were jumbled, almost like they were speaking a different language. Her brain rushed, processing the words before finally understanding the question and gave a nod.

Both men had blank faces and no distinguishing features. One of them pulled a pill bottle out of his pocket and popped it open, handing one of the brightly colored spheres over to her. Thyra looked at it and took it from them. She swallowed it down and in moments, the already foggy room became more hazy. Her eyes started to close. One of them scribbled again on his notepad, the other one watching intently.

"Thyra."

The room began to fade. Her body felt extremely light and a warmth crept up her spine.

"Thyra."

She felt herself falling slowly as if through thickened air.

"THYRA!"

Thyra's big green avian eyes snapped open in attention, staring at the ceiling, and she turned her head to find the vulture sitting next to her.

"Ah, there you are. You were moving a lot in your sleep." Aadhya stood and strolled into the kitchen, then opened the fridge.

Thyra's chest pounded, her heart still racing as she looked around the apartment once again. She rolled over onto her side, and held her head, closing her eyes for a second and taking a deep breath. "A dream."

"What was your dream about?" Aadhya asked from the kitchen, cracking open some eggs into a frying pan.

Thyra slowly rolled off the couch and stretched out her wings, her back arching towards the ceiling. She took a couple steps as she stretched her legs and went to sit on the opposite side of the kitchen's bar. "It's really fuzzy in my mind. There was a very bright room, and two guys in white coats."

Aadhya cracked another egg into the pan and glanced over at Thyra, her gaze serious. "It was of the labs then?"

Thyra looked away, trying to remember details. "Yeah, I guess it was."

There was a short silence as the smell of cooking eggs filled the small room. The aroma of coffee wafted alongside it, churning Thyra's already hungry stomach.

"My people believe in dreams," Aadhya said, turning her attention back to the eggs. She deftly flipped them with a spatula. "They all have meaning. The fact that you had dreams of the labs could determine something in your future."

Thyra's head cocked to the side in confusion. "Really? What could the dream mean?"

"I cannot say," Aadhya said with a slight shrug. She turned back to the fridge to grab a bowl of white rice and some flatbreads from it, along with a bottle of red paste with strange writing on the label. "Was your time in the labs bad, or good?"

"I don't know." Thyra shuffled her wings and roused her feathers, trying to think back to those days. "I was never harmed, and I never went hungry or was sick. I guess in a way they weren't bad, but I remember feeling lonely, lost, and depressed. What could that mean for my future?"

Aadhya nodded as Thyra spoke, putting the flatbreads

and rice onto two plates. She picked up the skillet with one of her large gray foreclaws and placed an egg on top of each pile of rice. "It could mean you will feel those feelings once again. Someone close could be lost and you could feel alone."

Aadhya gave a small chuckle to break the serious tone and picked up the bottle of red paste, scooping some out to put on each plate. She slid the dish over to Thyra and gave a warming beak grin to her new friend. "Or it could not mean anything at all. Just a dream from memories past."

"Well let's hope it doesn't mean shit," Thyra said with a frown. "Uh, no offense."

"None taken."

Thyra leaned closer to the plate in front of her. The red paste was very strong smelling and the many different spices and scents made her nares tingle. She reached out and brought it to her beak to taste it. Surprisingly, it was not as hot as she thought it would be. It was quite mild in fact.

Aadhya ate her own food and watched curiously as Thyra proceeded to devour her breakfast.

Thyra noticed her look. "I thought Hindu didn't eat eggs or meat,"

Aadhya shrugged and took a final bite, finishing up her meal. Bits of it had lodged in the black beard feathers hanging from her beak. "Some Hindu are very strict. I, however, am not."

Thyra stared at the pieces of food decorating the black feathers and motioned to her own beak. "You got a little..."

Aadhya's strong red and yellow eyes opened wide as she quickly grabbed a dish towel and wiped her beak with it, a little red showing around her nares. Thyra could not   help but laugh at the big gryphoness's bashfulness.

A timer beeped loudly in the kitchen, the coffee stopping its drip. Aadhya walked over to grab the pot and began to pour it into two coffee mugs sitting on the counter. This confused Thyra as well, remembering they had tea last night.

"So, coffee for the morning, and tea at night?"

"Is that not the way of things?" Aadhya replied curiously.

Thyra shrugged. "I meant I just figured you weren't a coffee type of bird."

The white gryphoness blinked. "At first, it was hard for me to get used to the black substance, but now I must admit I crave it in the mornings."

Thyra gave her a nod of acknowledgement and lifted the mug to her beak, taking a deep breath of the smoky fragrance. The sound of Thyra's ring tone filled the quiet room suddenly and she walked back into the living area to retrieve the phone. She looked down and, seeing it was Johnathen, said to Aadhya, "It's the husband."

The gryphoness smiled and went back to her own business, padding gently into her bedroom.

"Hey you...I slept well, you?...That's good...Yeah, Addy's place is really nice, super close to the stadium too... Yeah, my wings were aching last night. Still are sore, actually. I knew I couldn't make the flight home and back again this morning...Well, I will see how it goes today...If you wanted to...Ok! I'll call you after practice...Love you too, bye."

Thyra ended the call and looked at the screen, noticing a missed text from Isabell. She wondered what it could be about and went to open the message.

"He sounds nice," came Aadhya's voice from the other room.

Thyra closed the cell phone, deciding whatever Isabell wanted was probably not important at the moment. She went to retrieve her mug of abandoned coffee, finally taking a sip of the robust beverage.

"He is. Nicer than I deserve."

When Aadhya came out of the hallway, her feathers were no longer white. Her old plumage had been replaced by a bright coat of rusted orange and tan reds. Thyra's eyes widened at the different colored feathers and almost spit out her coffee.

"Addy? H...how did you change colors?"

"Makeup," she said matter-of-factly. "It is customary for my species to adorn ourselves in a special type of rich soil found in my country. I quite enjoy the colors myself."

Aadhya turned to walk in front of a large mirror in the kitchen. She turned this way and that, making sure her plumage was completely covered, dust pouring from her feathers as she ruffled them.

"I do this for special occasions, such as before a game."

Thyra set her empty mug down and raised an eye ridge. "But we aren't playing a game today. It's another practice day, right?"

The decorated gryphoness turned to Thyra with an almost wicked beak grin, excitement glowing in her impressive eyes. "Today, we have a scrimmage."

Isabell beat her wings gently in the cool autumn breeze, surveying the city's main park. There was a stage set up by the petite pond at the center and lots of outdoor benches. A few people were carrying supplies out of a moving truck with a cross painted on the side.

Patrol cars set around the city block redirected traffic away from the area. Isabell was too high up for anyone to take notice, allowing her plenty of time to spy on The Gathering.

Isabell ground her thin black beak with agitation and banked to the side to do another pass. She spied a couple priests in highly decorated robes and several well-dressed guests showing up early for the picnic. Many of the people held signs depicting drawings of gryphons with red X's, racist slander against minorities, and other fascist sayings.

American and Confederate flags were posted around a large white tent, presumably where the congregants would be gathering to eat.

She banked once again, heading away from the city center and back towards the pub. Minutes flew by quickly as her heart pounded away in her chest, both with anger and anxiety. Up ahead, she could see that the bar's parking lot was filled with cars and motorcycles. Isabell dove, tucking her wings in tight with her tail pointed straight back.

With a couple backwards wing beats, she was standing before Saul, Carl, and Johnathen.

"You didn't tell her?" Saul asked curiously, puffing on a cigarette. Johnathen hung up his phone and put it away in his pocket. "No, she seemed really preoccupied and I didn't want to worry her too much."

"So, I guess she's not coming." Isabell said, looking around at the crowd of people outside the bar. "Would have been nice to have at least one other gryphon with us."

"She's still up in Athens. Yesterday was the first day of gryphball practice and she was too tired to fly down last night. Plus, she couldn't miss the second day either. I don't want her giving up on the dream of being a gryphball player for a rally."

Johnathen was actually relieved that Thyra had not come home last night. He had spent the entire evening at the bar with Isabell and Saul, telling them everything he knew about The Gathering. Johnathen knew Thyra would have refused to go to practice and would be right there with them now. Surely it would have cost her the new position in her league.

Saul and Carl were wearing cut-off sleeve leather jackets and there was a large number of people with them. Most wore the same biker outfit that they did, but there were other groups scattered about.

Each group was representing various causes, not just for gryphons. Crowds of people wearing colorful shirts, flags of various natures, and a multitude of signs were conversing amongst themselves. Everyone seemed calm and ready for the impending confrontation, but upon closer inspection, Isabell could tell they were all very nervous.

"Well? How does it look?" Saul asked curiously, looking down at the small gryphon.

"About what we thought," she replied. "I would say fifty or so are there so far, but it is still early."

"You didn't see Matthew, did you?" Johnathen asked curiously, looking down at Isabell. She shook her head, "No, but I was too high up to pick out any noticeable faces."

"I doubt he's there. This isn't like him. Showing his true colors in public like this is a little too risky for that cunning asshole. He's probably hiding out somewhere, and if this all backfires, he'll claim he had nothing to do with it."

Saul nodded, and gave Carl a pat on the back. "Go ahead and get everyone ready."

Carl nodded and headed into a group of people in the parking lot. Saul pulled out a pack of cigarettes and took two out, offering one to Isabell. She gladly took it and waited as Saul presented the lighter. The gryphoness took a deep pull, and breathed out through her nares, smoke pouring from the slits on her beak.

"You ready?" Johnathen asked Isabell. She looked around at the crowd of gathered people, taking a mental count. "Yeah, I think this is everyone."

She jumped up on a newspaper stand in front of the bar's entrance, where everyone could see her. Then the petite gryphon took a deep breath and let out an ear-piercing screech, causing everyone in the area to immediately quiet down. They paid full attention to the colorful avian.

Isabell stood with her twilight-tinted chest feathers puffed up with authority. Her blue eyes scanned the crowd as she summoned up all her strength to speak to them. "Today is not a day for the faint of heart! Congregating in the park are those that wish to see us gone. Wish to see us dead! They hate us for who we are, but we are here, and we will not go quietly into the night!"

Inside, she was shaking with fear, but she showed no sign of it. She sat up straight, addressing each person in the crowd. "They call us faggots, niggers, and beasts! They shame us, and do everything in their power to convince others of outrageous lies. We have gone on for far too long living in the shadows, and today, we will show them what we are made of!"

The whole crowd began cheering, people shouting and clapping their hands. The energy of the mass raised her own spirits, finding new frantic energy as she resettled her wings.

"I haven't lived here very long, but I love this peaceful little city. I know a lot of you, and I know that for many of you this is your birthplace. We have let these fascists take over our town, and I say it's about damn time we shut them up! Now, who's with me?!"

Everybody cheered even louder which stirred a grin on Isabell's face. She savored the moment, all eyes on her as the crowd began to stir violently. Groups of people started to leave the parking lot, making their way down the street as they shouted or chanted along with one another. Isabell hopped down from the stand and walked back up to Saul, who could not help but laugh at the sudden confidence from the gryphon.

"Good speech. Seems it got everyone even more riled up."

Isabell watched as the last of the crowd moved into the street, disappearing over a small hill. "Maybe it was too much."

"Drastic times call for drastic measures," he replied. "Did you go out and get the video camera today?"

Isabell nodded and drew out a small but rugged looking video camera. "Yeah, hopefully I will get some good footage of one of their speeches. Or anything else to incriminate them."

"Just remember you need to get a shot that has The Gatherings logo in the background along with some of their signs." Johnathen reminded Isabell. "If you don't get it in one shot, they could discredit the footage and say it's fake."

"I'll get the shot." Isabell walked away toward the group of bikers with Saul and Carl. Johnathen walked over to his Mustang and started the engine, ready to go when they were. The bikers were all patiently waiting next to their motorcycles for Saul's command.

"You ready?" Saul asked.

Isabell took one last deep breath and nodded.

"Let's go."

Chapter 23 Contact

The loud rumbling of engines suddenly came to a halt just outside of town. Isabell landed swiftly among them and looked behind her to see crowds of people heading up the street.

Saul had put down his kickstand and relaxed back on his black chopper, turning his gaze on his fellow bikers. Johnathen had pulled up next to the bikers and shut off the Mustang along with everyone else. The gang members sat silently, nodding in acknowledgement as Saul went over the plan one more time.

"Just like we discussed," he said firmly. "My group will draw away the police between James Street and Twelfth. Carl's group will be on the east side of the square, creating a hole in the barricades so folks can get through easily." Saul looked over to Johnathen. "That pretty Mach-1 of yours will draw lots of attention. Just follow Carl's group and create a distraction. Roast the tires or somethin' like that."

Though Johnathen's hands were shaking, he laughed in response, keeping up a strong appearance in front of the bikers. "Yeah, I can do that."

Isabell felt a swell of unease about the dark looks on their faces and spoke up. "Remember, only get violent if they do first. This is supposed to be a peaceful protest. The goal is to make our presence known, and to get footage of their true colors"

"You hear her, boys? Peaceful." Saul looked around

to the group. He started up his engine first; smoke pouring from his exhaust while the thundering sound of a V-twin echoed through the street. Other bikes joined as did Johnathen, creating a roaring symphony of motors as they started up and accelerated down separate streets.

Isabell locked eyes with Saul one last time, seeing nothing but confidence in them, and then he was gone. She took to the air just as soon as the motorcycles pulled away, gaining altitude with hard wing strokes. The sun was high in the sky and its light beamed down on her iridescent feathers.

She briefly closed her eyes and enjoyed a moment of peace, thinking about how the rest of the country was probably just starting their morning without a care in the world. She yearned for her own people to be so carefree. Hopefully, the fight she would bring today would help pave the way for that reality and secure their future from violence.

Down below, she watched the groups of bikes make twists and turns through the city's small downtown. Their presence created an uproar. It didn't take them long to speed past the multiple cops blocking the entrances to the park. The law took the bait. Sirens flipped on and the patrol cars sped away after the bikers.

Isabell watched from up high as Saul's group led the police away, leaving the entrance to the park unguarded, except for a group of spectators. Johnathen pulled up in his Mustang, which made the crowd to focus their attention to him. He revved up the healthy V8 and let the rear end go, laying down rubber down the street. It was enough of a distraction that Carl's small team could approach the barricades unhindered. They pulled up and shut off their bikes, then started to work on clearing the barriers from the street. The protesters began pouring in from city alleyways to join them.

Isabell landed on the roof of a nearby building. She

drew out the video camera and held it up to her eyes, recording as much evidence as she could. A man garbed in a suit with blond hair stood on the stage centered in the park. He was passionate about his speech, pumping his fists into the air and pointing to people in the crowd. They joined in, waving their racist signs and shouting back.

"We have a plague in this town, one that infects all of us. There are man-made beasts, chinks, blacks, and Indians killing our perfect city. They water down and tinge our perfect white heritage. They tear down our monuments and make changes to history. They threaten our way of life and will ruin us if we do not stop them!"

Isabell could hear the speech but only faintly from where she sat. It could be from design so that the other spectators and news crews on the street could not hear them. She hoped the camera would pick up the audio as well.

The protesters poured in, waving their signs and shouting at the rally participants inside the park. The blond man on stage stopped his speech and pointed to the protesters pouring in. He shouted something, but it was all lost in the noise of hundreds of people yelling at one another. The two groups formed up facing each other, leaving a gap between them. The protesters began taking up chants and walking in circles. Many members of The Gathering picked up rocks and other objects to throw at the protesters. The protesters tried to protect themselves with their signs, but it was no use. A biker in the crowd lost his temper when a rock struck his head, and he immediately charged into the opposing rally members.

Everyone crowded into the fight, the two sides clashing as they went to back each other up. People swarmed around one another like ants on an anthill, throwing punches and kicks. Most of the protesters backed up as small fights broke out on the front lines and escalated into much bigger brawls.

Isabell could see that things were about to worsen and took a deep breath. She couldn't stay out of this part any longer. She put the camera away in her bag and jumped off the roof. She glided down to meet Carl and his team on the far side of the park. Down on the ground, the madness of it all put fear into the small gryphoness. The sound of people yelling, sirens blaring, and stones breaking car windows hit her with overwhelming force.

"Where's Saul?" she shouted to Carl, who looked around and then shook his head at Isabell.

She could see why he didn't know what was going on. It was chaos. News crews filmed the action, watching from afar as people punched, kicked, and threw things at each other. No one could tell who was whom anymore. The groups of fighting seemed to grow and move towards her rapidly. Her ear tufts pinned back in fear and she hunched down as a large group approached her. She felt helpless against the mass of towering people and tried to get away.

Someone tripped over her, the weight falling right on top of her frail body. She gasped, hitting the hard concrete, fighting for air as the wind was knocked out of her.

Carl rushed over to pick them up and helped Isabell to her feet once again. "Are you alright?"

She winced, feeling a sharp pain in her leg, which quickly numbed from the adrenaline setting in. "Yeah, I'm…"

A voice shouted from her left side. "They have a beast with them!"

Isabell's eyes opened wide. A group of rally participants advanced, pointing fingers at her. Carl's large frame stood in front of her and raised his fists. "Isabell, go," he said, his expression solid and unfazed.

She took one look at Carl. He had turned his attention

to the group rapidly approaching. One man stepped forward and threw a punch at Carl. He turned his body to one side, dodging the right hook to his face. Carl threw out a heavy left hook to counter; landing a solid hit on the man's face. He dropped to the ground, but another man stepped forward and landed a hit on Carl. The biker stumbled back a step then returned the hit, taking the others head on. But there were too many of them, and Carl quickly became overpowered. Two of the men turned their attention away from Carl and started to run towards Isabell.

Isabell turned tail and fled, sprinting away from them. There was not enough room to take flight between the people. They gave chase while she rushed through the sea of people, darting between their legs and feet.

She was so intent on making sure that she put distance between herself and her pursuers that she did not see the man being decked in front of her. He fell right on top of her, forcing a sharp shrill out of her beak. She squirmed, talons raking at the asphalt as she tried to pull herself free from the man's unconscious form.

Isabell turned her head back to find that her assailants had caught up with her. Her heart beat heavy in her chest, her fear spiking. Nevertheless, she was ready to fight.

A hand grabbed her by the scruff of her neck and pulled her out from underneath the unconscious body. Isabell let out a loud squawk and swiped her foreclaws blindly into the air, desperate to free herself. She felt her sharp talons rend the assailant's flesh causing him to yell out in pain. He dropped the gryphoness, and she landed on her feet.

"You demon! You'll pay for that!" the man shouted out, clutching his bleeding arm. She twisted and turned, lashing out furiously in all directions.

She got in a few satisfying slashes on their ankles before a heavy boot struck her chest. Isabell flew through the air and hit the concrete and gasped, struggling for air. Her chest felt like it was caved in, and she could hardly breathe. The small gryphoness coughed and wheezed as the two men walked closer. She screamed out in pain as a boot stepped on her wing, a loud snap echoing through her body.

One of the men grabbed her by the throat. She opened her eyes, weakly looking up at the hateful visage of her assailant. She scowled and hissed weakly as he drew his fist back.

"Say goodnight, you disgusting beast," he spat.

Then everything went black.

&♦

A loud whistle blew from the field below signaling the end of the practice. Thyra and her teammates stopped mid-flight and dove to the sidelines. The gryphons gathered around Coach Victor as he sat down and placed his clipboard next to him.

"Good hustle everyone. After lunch, we'll change things up. Thyra, Rachel, and Nathanial, you will run defense against Aadhya and Antonio. The rest of you will do weight training."

Thyra and Rachel looked to the glaring eyes of Nathanial, his dark brown eyes looking at them with disgust.

"Just stay out of my way," the arrogant gryphon said, tilting his beak into the air. He turned tail and walked away angrily, leaving the confused birds behind.

Thyra gave Rachel a dumbfounded look. "I wonder why he's so sour. We're on the same team!"

"Do not take it personally," Antonio said, standing next to the crimson dusted Aadhya. "Nathanial is not the friendly type."

"Yeah, we noticed that!" Rachel growled as she stood and ruffled her tawny feathers. "That stuck up caracara needs to lighten up!"

The four friends began walking back to the locker rooms with their teammates, but Thyra lagged behind, her footsteps slowing. She let out a groan and resettled her wings.

Aadhya noticed her discomfort and chuckled softly. She extended a gigantic wing comfortingly around Thyra. Aadhya cooed softly almost like a dove as she talked. "If you wish to stay with me again tonight, I have some herbs that will help ease the pain."

Thyra had planned on flying home that night and spending time with Johnathen, but with the way she was feeling at the moment, maybe staying at Aadhya's again would not be a bad idea. She smiled at her friend. "Thanks. I might take you up on that."

The locker room was busy with gryphons showering, changing clothes, and chatting about the day's events. Thyra settled in at her locker, perking her ears to the conversations of others. Most of them were talking about their own performances and what teams they had played for in the past, but there was one conversation that caught her attention.

"...Apparently those extremists were having a protest, or a rally of sorts."

"Yeah, I heard a lot of people got hurt, and a gryphoness too."

"No shit? I didn't know there were any of us down in that little city. Where was it? Macon?"

Thyra's heart hammered, panic filling her head as she whipped around to face the two corvid gryphons talking among each other. "Did you hear a name?"

One of the gryphons blinked in surprise at her

outburst, but the other simply shook his head, still looking down at his phone and browsing through the story. "No. It just happened a little while ago. They're still clearing it all up."

Thyra opened her locker, dug out her phone and turned it back on. The device lit up and buzzed with messages from all sorts of people she knew, all of them posting links to the news article. She also had several missed calls from Johnathen, and she was about to call him back when she saw that one text from Isabell that Thyra had ignored that morning.

Thyra, I know that you're not usually for this stuff, but we are protesting those crazy church bastards this evening. If you could come and show support, it would be welcomed, but I understand if you are busy. Please get back to me soon! Isabell.

"Thyra?" Antonio walked over to her, noticing the gryphoness was in great distress. "Is something wrong?"

Thyra choked down tears of panic and looked back at the maroon-colored gryphon. "I...I think my friend is in a lot of trouble."

His brow tightened in concern. "Do you think it is serious?"

"Yes. She was at an anti-gryphon protest in Macon." Thyra's voice trembled. "I think she's been badly hurt."

Aadhya and Rachel moved in closer, having heard that last part.

"Thyra . . ." said Rachel, her wings fluttering in concern.

Thyra took a deep breath as she collected her thoughts and then started grabbing her things from the locker. "I need to go."

"I will assist you." Aadhya said, standing tall,

confidence in her foreign voice.

"Yeah! I'm not leaving you behind either!" Rachel chirped up, resettling her feathers with a big grin.

"I, too, will follow," Antonio said with a supporting smile.

Thyra glanced at all three of them, bewildered that they would suddenly leave with her. Tears welled in her eyes and her spirits rose, finding comfort in the compassion of her new friends.

A moment later, the coach walked into the locker room, his eyes on the four anxious gryphons talking in the corner. Victor gave them stern looks. "Is there something going on here?"

Thyra approached the gigantic gryphon, taking in a deep breath. "There's been an emergency, and I need to leave."

Victor looked down at Thyra, seeing her distress, but adopted his usual dead stare. "Leave if you must, but there will be punishment for missing practice."

Rachel ran up to stand next to Thyra, earning a raised eye ridge out of Victor. "Well you're going to punish us all then! Because we're going with Thyra to help.'

The other two stepped forward and the coach glanced at all of them. He took a deep breath and let out a sigh, his stern manner briefly lifting. "Fine. But you had better return tomorrow and be here two hours early. Understood?"

"Yes sir!" the band replied in unison.

Victor breathed out through his nares, much like a horse snorting with fake agitation. "Be careful," he said quietly. "Dismissed."

They all turned and headed for their lockers, gathering personal belongings before barreling out the locker room door.

Chapter 24 Consequence

"Johnathen...Yes, I read all about it on the news. Why wouldn't you tell me..? Yeah, I would have been there for her! This is more important than gryphball practice!...Yes, I forgive you, but … Do you know what all happened?...Is she alright?...Ok call me when you find out more…Love you too…"

Thyra closed her phone and put it away in her pouch.

"How much longer, Thyra?" Rachel groaned in an annoying chirp as her little wings beat hard against the headwind. "Feels like we have been flying for hours. My flight from Chattanooga isn't even this far away!"

The little gryphoness had a point. Usually the flight was much quicker, but the head wind had been giving them trouble for the past half hour.

"We should see the city in five or ten minutes." Thyra assured her.

"Do you have a plan?" Aadhya asked.

Aadhya was the only one who had no issues flying into the head wind. Her much broader and greater wingspan made easy work of the short trip. Aadhya seemed to glide like a kite with only the occasional wing beat from her massive peppered wings. Antonio had moved in next to Thyra, timing his wing beats with her own.

Thyra's eyes narrowed. The sadness and fear that had welled within her had slowly transformed into rage. "If members of The Gathering are still in the park, then we drive them out. No one hurts my friends and gets away with it."

She had spent the journey thinking back to all the times she had ignored the many names they called her, their oppression, what they put Johnathen through, and now this rally. Gathering people together against minorities? Banding together for the purpose of doing harm? Enough was enough.

Antonio could see this new energy in Thyra's eyes, and decided it was best to leave her be. He fell back and went to join Aadhya. "She really seems set on fighting these extremists."

Aadhya gave another powerful wing stroke and looked over to Antonio. "I do not believe violence will solve violence, but there are some that cannot be reasoned with. If what Thyra says is true, these people seem to be beyond diplomacy."

Antonio looked ahead and reluctantly agreed with what she had to say. He was not the fighting or aggressive type, but he would stand by them.

Aadhya's eartufts perked up, hearing noises in the distance. "Sirens. I will scout ahead!"

With a few hard wing beats, she accelerated past the band and flew fast towards the city. Thyra watched her pass, surprised at the alarming speed she was able to suddenly pick up. The larger gryphon left the rest of the band behind in an instant.

They all picked up the pace as well and as the city came into Thyra's view, Aadhya returned. "It looks as though it is done, Thyra. There seems to be nothing we can do."

Thyra ground her beak, clicking with agitation as she pushed hard forward, still fueled by anger.

The rally and protest had come to an end, and all there was left was cleaning up the carnage. Police cars buzzed through the streets as crowds of people watched from behind barricades. The park was littered with signs and trash.

Ambulances carried out the unconscious or seriously injured, while police forces threw cuffs onto whomever they could catch. News channel teams stood at the boundary lines, getting interviews from the witnesses.

Thyra looked for a little violet gryphoness, but all she saw was people. She dove suddenly, throwing her friends off guard as she barreled towards the earth. With a quick backstroke, she landed outside one of the barriers, causing an uproar from the onlookers behind it. The rest of the gryphons quickly followed, landing in next to her. Bright lights flashed as everyone started to take pictures.

News reporters ran up to them, asking questions and causing Aadhya to fling open her massive wings to push them back. She stood as tall as any human on all fours, which intimidated the reporters.

Thyra let out a loud screech, causing the people to wince and hold their ears. Once everyone had settled down, Thyra picked out one of the local news reporters that looked familiar and glared at him. "You! Tell me what happened here."

The reporter looked shocked, never have seeing more than one gryphon at a time so close up, and certainly not a group as grand as theirs.

"W...well, The Gathering was here today hosting an outdoor sermon, and there was some disagreement of their views. Protesters showed up, and a fight broke out. At the moment we don't know who started it or why. I was hoping perhaps you could shed some light on the situation."

Thyra took a couple steps towards the reporter with a grim look, making him cower and grip his microphone tighter.

"Disagreement of their views?! Do you not know what those people want? They want genocide! They hate us, and anyone that is different! That's not a disagreement of views, what they want is outright inhumane!" Thyra shouted, glaring at the camera and the crowd.

Another reporter stepped forward. "Were you a part of the protest?"

Thyra felt a deep compulsion to claw his greedy eyes out, but she could see that anger and aggression was not going to get her far. She forced her voice to calm.

"N...no, but I should have been." She pointed at the rest of the crowd with a curved talon. "All of us should have been. We need to fight these people with everything we have. Don't you see what Matthew has been preaching about? What him and his followers want in the end? They want this city to be eradicated of everyone who doesn't agree with their views! He wants to drive away everyone that isn't a white human. He has pulled wool over everyone's eyes and turned his congregation into a bigoted mass of hatred. He doesn't want anything that is good for our city, and we can't just let him have it. No matter how much money or power he has, we have to fight him with everything we've got!"

Thyra's friends were judging the crowd. Some people seemed to understand and talked amongst themselves in agreement. There were some that were upset with Thyra's words and began to yell at her.

"How dare you disgrace Bishop Matthew like that!" "You are the ones we need to fight against!"

Antonio walked up beside Thyra, noting that police officers that were gathering around them, sensing another bout of violence could begin. "We need to go..."

Thyra looked away from the reporters and swallowed nervously, realizing what kind of position she just put her friends in. Some of the officers had hands on their weapons, ready to act if any of them posed a threat. She turned back to the original reporter she had spoken to.

218

"Where did they take the injured?"

"East Medical." He replied quickly.

Thyra turned and nodded to her friends, who all quickly took wing into the sky, stirring up dust and trash as they climbed away from the street.

Rachel beat her wings hard to keep pace with Thyra "Man you really gave it to them back there! I was so shaken up, I couldn't say anything! It's probably a good thing Aadhya was there, or those cops would have been on top of us in no time."

Aadhya and Antonio fell in behind the two, following Thyra towards the outskirts of town. Aadhya was calm and conformed as ever, not a single feather out of place or any qualm in her voice. "I did not wish to be viewed as a menace, but my size is opportune at times."

"Thanks guys..." Thyra said to them, knowing the decision to face the crowd was foolish. She looked forward now, spying the small hospital in the distance.

"I do hope your friend is alright." Antonio said.

Thyra descended towards the crowded parking lot of the hospital.

"She will be."

Epilogue

Isabell's blue avian eyes slowly opened. Her vision was fuzzy, but she could make out figures standing around her. Their voices were muffled, sounding like they were speaking from underwater.

She glanced around, the bright light growing dimmer as her focus came back. Her hearing improved enough to make out the soft beeping of the heart monitor. She looked down at her beak, noticing the tubes hanging from it protruding from her nares. She tried to move, but her chest and wings were bound in a hard material.

Thyra was over in the corner of the small hospital room, sitting and talking with Johnathen and three unfamiliar gryphons. Thyra stopped talking as she saw Isabell attempting to move and walked over to her.

"Good morning, sleepy head." Thyra said with a faint beak grin.

Isabell's eyes wandered around the room, taking in the familiar faces as well as the new ones. "W…where am I?" she asked, still out of it. She tried to move once again and winced at the tight pain in her chest.

Thyra placed a foreclaw on Isabell's chest gently. "You're safe. That's all that matters. Now rest, don't try to move."

Isabell relaxed once again and took a deep breath, her eyes focusing on the new gryphons' faces. One of them, a handsome male, took a step forward and gave a polite bow of his head. "A shame we must meet like this. I am Antonio. This is Rachel and Aadhya."

Johnathen walked up behind Thyra and placed a hand on her shoulders looking down at the injured gryphoness. "How are you feeling?" he asked.

Isabell looked to the new gryphons and back up at Johnathen. "Everything feels tight. How bad is it?"

Thyra's ear tufts pinned back and she looked away for a second, not wanting to be the bearer of bad news. Isabell frowned and glanced over to see her wing outstretched, wrapped in a tight cast and hanging by wires. The heart monitor started to beep faster as Isabell looked at her mangled wing. Thyra hesitated for a minute, "The doctor said it's broken in three different locations. They did all they can, but…"

"They think I may never fly again, don't they . . ?" Tears rolled down Isabell's cheeks.

Johnathen squeezed Thyra's shoulders while the other gryphons looked away, not knowing Isabell well enough to get involved.

"They are not sure… but I believe you can." Thyra looked down at the smaller violet gryphoness, trying to smile once again to keep a positive attitude. "They already have you booked for therapy classes for the next several months and the doctor seemed optimistic."

Isabell remained silent, staring at her deformed wing wrapped tightly in the cast. She tried to move it, but found it was bound well. Her claws went to her chest, finding it covered in a similar cast. "And what of this. What else is wrong!" Isabell shouted, and turned to look at Thyra, tears still rolling from her eyes.

Thyra winced. Isabell had every right to be angry, upset, and frightened. To take away a gryphon's flight was to take away their freedom. Thyra spilled out everything she knew in one go. "Four broken ribs, one bruised lung, a dislocated wing shoulder, and your right hindleg is fractured."

Isabell looked away again, choking back more tears. Everyone sat silent. The clock on the wall ticked for what seemed hours. The beeping of the heart monitor slowly turned back to normal and the oxygen machine breathed a puff of fresh air every couple seconds.

"I'm going to find the bastards that did this, and I'll rip their eyes out with my own claws." Isabell threatened softly.

Rachel jumped on the couch in the far side of the room and clicked on the television on the wall with a remote. "Well, that's going to be a little hard for you. As much as I would like to see you kick some ass, everyone involved in the rally was arrested today," Rachel flipped the television onto the news.

The same newscaster who'd interviewed Thyra at the scene was on camera. She was walking around the now clean park and talking about what took place. Occasionally scenes of police cars in the background with several people in handcuffs would show up while she narrated. Rachel turned up the volume on the television.

"… and nobody knows the real reason behind the violence earlier this morning. We have reason to believe it was The Gatherings motive to start the violent riot. Although the leader of The Gathering, Bishop Matthew, has stated otherwise."

The scene cut to an interview with Matthew at his desk, sitting calmly and looking proper. "I would never encourage my people to perform such acts of violence. I had no clue that this social event was even taking place. I can assure you, these bigots are not true members of The Gathering. I suspect that the Klan is behind this awful display of white supremacy."

Johnathen frowned in anger at seeing Matthew on the television once more. "I told you that he would deny everything if this went south."

The scene cut back to the newscaster once again, standing in the park's center. "When we pressed for further answers from the bishop, he had no comment. In the wake of what happened here this morning, we did have an interview with local gryphon who was not involved with the incident."

The footage cut to Thyra's speech, and Isabell perked her ear tufts at seeing Thyra on the television. The band of gryphons all smiled and turned to look at Thyra as the footage rolled on. Thyra fluffed her feathers out proudly, seeing that she had actually given a good speech. After her speech, the program cut to commercial.

"I hope you got through to the public," Isabell said, lying still and staring at the television. She looked to Johnathen suddenly. "What happened to my video camera?"

"I have it." Johnathen said.

Isabell let out a deep sigh of relief. "How did you find my bag?"

"After my part in the distraction, I went to go meet up with Saul as we planned, but he never showed up. I feared the worst and took alleys on foot to the park. The fighting had died down, and many cops were out arresting people. I looked for you and Carl, but I found your bag instead. Seems that camera is really robust, because your bag was beat up pretty bad."

Johnathen went on with his story. "I made it back to my car and looked over the footage. The speech that blond guy gave is exactly what we need. I haven't had time to make a copy, but when I do, I'm taking it directly to the press."

Isabell took a deep breath and relaxed. "If this makes the people realize what The Gathering's true colors are, it will all be worth it."

"It seems there were some that listened to Thyra, but a few were angered by her accusations." Aadhya pointed out. She was sitting in the back corner of the room, trying to minimize the amount of space she was taking up. "I have observed humans tend to deny reason, even with the correct evidence. Some do not accept truth and would rather take what they believe to the grave," she added as Rachel turned off the television.

"You may be right. It's going to take more than a protest to convince the most stubborn of those idiots." Johnathen chimed in. "But I think most of them will listen to reason. The Gathering doesn't have as strong a grip on the people as Matthew things."

"I may be new to all this, but I think I may have an idea!" Rachel chirped. The group turned to look at her as she smiled, bubbly as ever. "Well, in Chattanooga, we don't have anything like The Gathering. It's all traditional, like Baptists, Methodist, Catholic, and the like. Sure, there are some people up in the surrounding areas like Sand Mountain that are supposedly part of the KKK and what not, but nothing like a big organized cult that's out in the open. But what I was thinking is what if we made some sort of new hangout. Like a big club! Nothing like a new religion or church or cult, but something like our own version of The Gathering! We could make it for everyone and do a lot more fun activities." She rambled on, spit balling ideas to the group. Everyone was lost in thought, thinking for a minute.

"You mean play Matthew at his own game?" Johnathen thought out loud.

Rachel shrugged her wingshoulders. "I don't know

who Matthew is, but yeah! Sure!"

"The older guy on the news, in the interview."
Johnathen stared at Rachel who wore a blank expression.
"The guy who is in charge of the cult? Calls himself bishop
of The Gathering?" Johnathen continued to explain to her.
"We've been talking about him this whole time."

A light bulb seemed to go off in Rachel's little
head. "Oh! The old ugly guy in the pajamas. Got it. Yeah
he doesn't seem cool."

Johnathen rubbed his temples and let out a sigh.
"Yeah, that guy."

"I do see some possibilities in Rachel's idea."
Antonio said gently. "In Mexico, they would have such a
thing for the children. Parents from all around would bring
their children to meet and discuss life events as well. They
are tight-knit communities that help one another."
Everyone began to nod, their own ideas racing in their
minds and Antonio perked up as another idea occurred to
him. "Why not make it a gryphball club? We could host
weekly meetups with gryphball players. Host events and
raffles for tickets."

"I'm sure I could organize something like that,"
Thyra said with confidence.

She turned to look at Isabell who had been quiet for
some time now. Isabell was sound asleep, lying peacefully,
which brought a smile to Thyra's beak. Everyone else took
notice of the sleeping gryphoness and tip-toed into the hall.

Johnathen shut the door quietly behind them.
"Guys, it was nice to meet you but it's getting late, and it's
been a long day," he said, looking to all the gryphons.

"Likewise. A pleasure to meet you too, even if it
was not under the most ideal conditions." Antonio said and
reached up to shake Johnathen's hand.

Aadhya, standing as tall as Johnathen, bowed. "A

pleasure indeed. Hopefully will not be our last meeting."

Rachel jumped up on Thyra's back and held out her tiny foreclaws. "Yeah! I hope we get to hang out when all this blows over!" She reached up to shake Johnathen's finger.

"I'm sure we will all meet again." Johnathen replied with a smile.

Aadhya turned to Thyra. "I assume you will not be returning with us this evening?" Thyra gave a nod in response. "Then we will see you tomorrow for practice. Remember, Victor said we must come in early."

"I remember. I'll be there," Thyra replied. "Tonight, I just want to go home."

Aadhya nodded in agreement. "There is no place like home." She turned to look at the rest of the band. "I believe an exit from the roof is the easiest, yes?" They all nodded and turned to leave, heading for the stairs.

Rachel jumped off Thyra's back. "Six A.M., Thyra! Don't forget!" Rachel turned back and yelled as she dashed to follow the group.

Johnathen put his arm around Thyra and they headed to the elevator. "They seem like a good group of friends." He punched the elevator call button. "Especially for people you just met yesterday."

Thyra nodded in agreement and stepped in the elevator as it opened. "I've never met anyone like them." The elevator doors closed, and she let out a loud sigh. "It's good to have new friends. I think they are here to stay."

"Good, because we need all the help we can get." Johnathen said. "But you know what I really need?"

"What's that?" Thyra perked her eartufts and looked up at him.

"A stiff drink."

Alexander Bizzell

Made in the USA
Middletown, DE
18 January 2019